THE KILLER MOUNTAINS

Books by George G. Gilman available from New English Library:

ADAM STEELE 1: THE VIOLENT PEACE
ADAM STEELE 2: BOUNTY HUNTER
ADAM STEELE 3: HELL'S JUNCTION
ADAM STEELE 4: VALLEY OF BLOOD
ADAM STEELE 5: GUN RUN
ADAM STEELE 6: THE KILLING ART
ADAM STEELE 7: CROSS-FIRE
ADAM STEELE 8: COMANCHE CARNAGE
ADAM STEELE 9: BADGE IN THE DUST
ADAM STEELE 10: THE LOSERS
ADAM STEELE 11: LYNCH TOWN
ADAM STEELE 12: DEATH TRAIL
ADAM STEELE 13: BLOODY BORDER
ADAM STEELE 14: DELTA DUEL
ADAM STEELE 15: RIVER OF DEATH
ADAM STEELE 16: NIGHTMARE AT NOON
ADAM STEELE 17: SATAN'S DAUGHTERS
ADAM STEELE 18: THE HARD WAY
ADAM STEELE 19: THE TARNISHED STAR
ADAM STEELE 20: WANTED FOR MURDER
ADAM STEELE 21: WAGONS EAST
ADAM STEELE 22: THE BIG GAME
ADAM STEELE 23: FORT DESPAIR
ADAM STEELE 24: MANHUNT
ADAM STEELE 25: STEELE'S WAR: THE WOMAN
ADAM STEELE 26: STEELE'S WAR: THE PREACHER
ADAM STEELE 27: STEELE'S WAR: THE STOREKEEPER
ADAM STEELE 28: STEELE'S WAR: THE STRANGER
ADAM STEELE 29: THE BIG PRIZE
ADAM STEELE 30: THE KILLER MOUNTAINS

EDGE MEETS ADAM STEELE: TWO OF A KIND

THE KILLER MOUNTAINS

George G. Gilman

NEW ENGLISH LIBRARY

for
Stan and Joy
whose empty bottles mark
some of my back trails

A New English Library Original Publication, 1982

First NEL Paperback Edition April 1982

NEL Books are published by
New English Library,
Barnard's Inn, Holborn,
London EC1N 2JR, a division of Hodder and Stoughton Ltd.

Typeset by Rowland Phototypesetting Ltd.
Bury St Edmunds, Suffolk
Printed in Great Britain by
Collins, Glasgow.

British Library C.I.P.

Gilman, George G.
The killer mountains.—(Adam Steele; no. 30)
I. Title II. Series
823'.914[F] PR6058.A686/
ISBN 0-450-05377-6

CHAPTER ONE

THE MAN who stood on the fringe of a large expanse of timber, gazing impassively on as a band of Paiutes directed a hail of rifle fire at a line of six stalled wagons, looked almost entirely out of place in the landscape that surrounded him.

For he was dressed in a pale blue suit with a velvet trimmed collar on the jacket, a yellow vest and a lace-fronted white shirt. Only the black Stetson and riding boots were exactly right for a man in the Big Belt Mountains of Montana up toward the north-eastern end of the American Rockies. Maybe, too, the black buckskin gloves that fitted his hands so snugly.

And the fact that every item of his clothing was the worse for wear, suggesting he had been away from cities for a long time: in the kind of country where opportunities to replace ill-used clothes or clean off ingrained trail dust were few and far between.

His face, too, betrayed the first impression of a man out of his element. Especially when he was watching so implacably what appeared to be the prelude to wholesale slaughter.

It was the face of a man approaching forty. With deeply tanned and heavily lined skin that revealed most of his life had been spent out of doors and far away from city comforts. The features were regular, ruggedly good looking at his present age: but founded on a basic bone structure that in earlier times would have given an impression of weakness.

The eyes were coal black, the mouthline gentle in repose, the jaw firm. He was newly shaved this morning and did not wear a beard or moustache. He did maintain long sideburns, prematurely iron grey like the neatly trimmed hair on his head – showing just a trace of the auburn colouring of his youth.

He was slightly over five and a half feet tall and built on lean lines: the way he held and carried himself hinting at the compact strength commanded by his physique.

His name was Adam Steele.

And if the Indian attack ended the way it was shaping up to do, the resulting slaughter he was about to witness would be nothing new to him.

While he watched, he sweated. But the beads of salt moisture squeezing from his pores were caused entirely by the heat of mid-morning. And he used a grey silken scarf to mop at his sheened face, then hung it back around his neck and tucked the two diagonally weighted corners under the lapels of his jacket.

Furthermost from his mind was the fact that this oriental weapon of strangulation was of no use against the whooping and hollering Paiutes. Likewise the throwing knife which was stowed in a boot sheath, accessible to his gloved hand through a slit in the outside seam of his right pants leg. He did not wear a gunbelt or carry a concealed handgun.

Over a range of perhaps three quarters of a mile he could have done some damage with the Colt Hartford revolving rifle that rested in the boot on the saddle of his grey gelding waiting ten yards back in the pine trees.

But this was not his fight. And the people cowering inside the line of Conestoga wagons were not themselves mounting any kind of defence against the Indians who were closing in for the kill. Unless they had some plan that required the Paiutes to gallop their ponies into point-blank range.

And, abruptly, the Indians suspected something of the kind themselves: ceased firing their repeaters and brought their mounts to a rearing, snorting halt. Stared at the string of wagons and then anxiously in other directions. Seemingly only now realising that not a single shot had been exploded toward them in response to their onslaught.

Adam Steele was halfway up the southern slope of a narrow valley: had been brought to the fringe of the pine trees by the opening burst of gunfire. Reached his vantage point in time to see the ten buckskin-clad attackers racing their mounts out of rocky cover at the foot of the slope. To hit at a single flank of the short wagon train which had been heading west. And which, during the short time he watched, seemed to be totally deserted of human life.

But obviously there were people aboard the Conestogas. Drivers, at least, who had hauled on the reins to halt the four-horse teams when the initial fusillade of rifle fire shattered the mountain stillness to threaten equine panic. Then had scrambled into the insubstantial shelter of the wagons' canvas covers: to crouch behind the timbered sides as bullets cracked and thudded and ricochetted close by.

A tactic which suddenly worried the Paiutes. Who had curtailed their violent advance some fifty feet short of their objective. Now sat astride their heavily breathing ponies in a straggled line: nervously aware that the wagons, menacingly silent, provided the closest cover.

From the way in which the worried braves kept glancing at one of their number it was obvious he was their leader. And he was as concerned as the others: like them, constantly raked his suspicious gaze and the barrel of his Winchester along the line of bullet-scarred wagons. With fleeting looks up and down the valley and over his shoulder.

If words were exchanged, they were not spoken loud enough to carry to Adam Steele. And when a burst of shouting erupted from the throats of the braves, he could only guess at the sense of what was being said: from the way in which rifles were raked to aim at a single target but fingers were stayed on the triggers.

The cause of the excitement and the target for the ten repeaters was a piece of white fabric thrust out over the tailgate of the lead wagon: just a hand and a forearm exposed to wave the makeshift flag of truce.

The Indians became silent: momentarily looking like a lifesize carved tableau as they sat astride their ponies, Winchesters levelled from their shoulders. Then their leader canted his rifle to his shoulder and used his heels to signal his mount to advance a yard or so from the line.

'You wish to surrender to us, white men?' he called.

His English was good, marred by a gruff accent. The surrounding silence enabled his words to carry clearly to Adam Steele.

'We wish not to fight you! We wish to give you what you require in friendship! There is no necessity for violence and bloodshed! May I show myself without fear of –'

The leader of the braves interrupted the elderly-sounding man with a single word in his native tongue: in a tone that indicated an angry curse. Then: 'You talk of friendship, white man! There can be no friendship without trust! Without honour! We are of the Paiute nation! You have shown a flag of truce!'

His words were heavy with contempt.

The line of braves in back of him were gazing and aiming their rifles in all directions again: even more suspicious of a possible trap now. But all of them zeroed in on the same target again as the piece of white fabric was withdrawn. And a leg was swung out over the tailgate of the lead wagon: a rump and then another leg, the back, shoulders and head of the spokesman for the people aboard the Conestogas.

A man dressed entirely in black, except for a short arc of white clerical collar at his throat. The hair which was clipped very short to his hatless head was also white. He was tall and thin and slightly stooped at the shoulders.

Over such a distance, Adam Steele was unable to see his face in detail. From the white hair, stooped shoulders and slowness of his movements received an impression that the man was older than his voice had suggested. Close to seventy, perhaps.

The priest advanced across half the distance between his wagon and the band of Paiutes with his hands held out in front of him, palms upwards and fingers splayed. All ten Indians watched him fixedly until he came to a halt. Then complied with an order from their leader to cover the silent wagons. There was a brief exchange between the priest and the top brave, their voices pitched at a normal conversational level so that Steele could not hear what was said. Then the priest turned his back on the Indians and began to shout.

'Be not afraid of them, my followers! They ask only for a share of our food! Step down from your wagons to show that we do not bear arms! They were driven to attack us by hunger, and past experience with whites who regard all Indians as hostile savages!'

Tentatively, men and women emerged from the wagons. Some climbing over the tailgates and others appearing through the canvas flaps behind the high seats. All of them distrustful of the Paiutes with levelled rifles. Most of them fearful – some visibly quaking.

A young woman from the lead wagon. A middle-aged man and woman from the second in line. A younger couple and two teenage boys from the next. From the fourth Conestoga an even younger man and woman who kept their hands clasped despite the difficulty this gave them in climbing down to the ground. Two elderly women and an older man from the next wagon in the line. And from the final rig another middle-aged couple and a man in his mid-twenties.

Everybody dressed in hard-wearing work clothes: like they were farming people, except for the preacher. They stood nervously beside their wagons, the woman from the lead wagon in lonely isolation while the couples and families huddled close together.

The priest nodded his satisfaction with the result of his request. Spoke a few words of reassurance to the people and then returned his attention to the leader of the Paiutes. Who in turn said something to the braves behind him, which caused them to boot their Winchesters and follow his actions to dismount from their ponies.

But the tension remained high down on the floor of the valley, as the Indians moved away from their ponies and booted rifles. For each brave wore a weapons belt hung with a revolver, knife and tomahawk. And each stalked rather than walked, obviously poised to kill at close quarters if the situation demanded it. While it was apparent that the whites knew this.

The exceptions to these attitudes were seen in the demeanour of the priest and the Paiute leader. For both seemed to accept the truce at face value – trusting each other and confident they had the authority to dictate the actions of their followers.

Adam Steele could hear voices now, but none was raised sufficiently for the words to reach him clearly. And he watched for just a few more moments as, on the instruction of the priest, the whites began to offload some of their supplies from the wagons: and the braves took what was offered, transferring it to the pouches slung from the saddles on the ponies. Then, his face showing nothing of what he thought about events down on the valley floor, he turned and went back to where his horse was hitched to a clump of brush.

Within the pine forest that cloaked this slope of the valley, it was very quiet and the screen of thickly growing trees acted to mute whatever sounds were being made by the whites and the Indians below. Just as earlier the timber had masked the clop of hooves and creak of axles of the wagon train moving along the valley as Steele rode unhurriedly toward it: totally unaware that he was not alone in this area of the mountains until the first volley of rifle shots shattered the stillness of the pine fragrant air.

Now he unhooked a canteen from the horn of his Western saddle and squatted down on a fallen trunk. To take a drink, run a jacket sleeve across his sweat-tacky brow and wait for the business in the valley to be concluded. For a business deal was undoubtedly what it was. A trade, the outcome of which depended not on trust, honour or friendship. Instead, on the temperament of the brave who led the Paiutes. The lives of the priest and his followers in exchange for whatever the Indians decided they wanted to take from them. Unless the top man of the Paiutes demanded something that was not available or was simply toying with the whites. In which case the trade was merely for a few more minutes of life.

And if this was the outcome, Steele decided as he recorked the canteen and stood up from the fallen length of rotting tree, he had no intention of intervening. To put his own life at risk in an attempt to save a bunch of people crazy enough to travel these dangerous mountains without a gun between them.

Alternatively, he would sit it out up here in the cool, sweet-smelling shade until the Indians took their peaceful leave of the whites. Then ride down into the valley and along the westbound trail for which he had been looking for two days: ignoring the carnage of a massacre or tipping his hat to the people aboard the wagons as he passed them. In no hurry. Enjoying the peace and the loneliness and the beauty of the northern mountains. With a fine horse under him, saddlebags well stocked with supplies and an adequate stake of bounty money to buy whatever he needed in the next town he happened to enter.

There had been no trouble that concerned him for several months now as he rode at an easy pace northwards up through the eastern Rockies. From the Sangre de Cristo Mountains of Colorado Territory, through Wyoming and into Montana. With brief stopovers at Denver and Laramie and a small town called Three Forks on the Yellowstone River. No trouble that concerned anybody until this morning, when the first burst of repeater rifle fire caused him to rein in the grey gelding and swing down from the saddle.

It had been a more sporadic crackle of gunfire that had embroiled him in a violent search for a fortune in hidden money down in the south of Colorado Territory. The prize that had attracted him then had been the biggest one he was ever offered – and lost, if he did not count his birthright. And also discounted those very few people who had been near and dear to him.

But having lost so much in the past, he was able to accept philosophically that he was not destined to share in a million dollars cash. And, during his long and lonesome ride toward no predetermined destination, he felt not a moment's regret or resentment that his ruling fate had cheated him yet again. What he did feel was a new strength of purpose, founded on the resolve that in the future he would not put his life on the line unless he was one hundred per cent certain of the reward he was aiming for.

And right here and now in the Big Belt Mountains of Montana, he required only to get down on to that easy riding trail in the valley. But there was no rush. And certainly no need to involve himself with the potentially lethal situation beside the stalled wagon train.

He hooked the canteen back on the horn of the saddle and ran a gloved hand gently down the nose of the gelding.

A man shouted with shrill anger.

Several women screamed.

A revolver shot cracked.

The gelding snorted softly.

Adam Steele murmured in his easy Virginian drawl: 'Easy, feller. Seems our wait could be over, but I'm not looking to get into any heavy action.'

CHAPTER TWO

THERE WERE stretched seconds of utter silence in the wake of the gunshot. Then a burst of loud talk, curtailed by a single voice shouting louder than the rest.

Just as when the fusillade of rifle fire had surprised him earlier, Adam Steele had to consciously suppress the impulse to draw the Colt Hartford from the boot. And advanced empty-handed to the vantage point he used a few minutes ago. Came within clear sight and sound of what was happening in the valley just as the elderly priest commanded his frightened and angry followers into a renewed silence. And turned from looking at them to gaze at the Paiutes who were now in a close-knit group by their ponies, a woman held captive by two of the braves. While their leader aimed a revolver at the priest, who was holding out his arms again in a gesture of supplication.

If anybody had been hit by the gunshot, the victim was still on his or her feet.

'You said you required just food, White Fox!' the distraught priest pleaded in a shrill tone.

The brave who aimed a gun at him over a range of six feet replied in a low voice. And what he said caused a young man to lunge from out of the bunch of whites gathered behind the priest.

'You're not gonna take Wilma!' he shrieked.

The two Indians who held the woman stepped backwards and dragged her with them. While the others snatched the handguns from their weapons belts.

'John!' This from a woman in the group of whites: the calling of the name giving sound to the terror that gripped the huddle of people.

John came to an abrupt halt as gun barrels swung to aim at him. And was immobile as he listened to something being said to him – the direction in which he and the other whites stared revealing to Steele that it was the captive Wilma who was speaking.

The priest nodded in agreement with what she said, then added something of his own. Which caused John to turn and move disconsolately back to the group.

White Fox spoke and again the priest nodded. All the revolvers were replaced on the weapons belts and the Paiutes got astride their ponies. Wilma was offered assistance to climb up behind one of the braves and she accepted it meekly. Then the Indians urged their horses forward: heading them westwards along the valley floor. At an easy canter which raised an elongated billow of grey dust.

The captive woman, clinging tightly to the brave, glanced backwards just once. And perhaps saw through the dust the scene at the side of the line of wagons – as the priest turned toward his followers, dropped to his knees and they did likewise. Hands were clasped in front of chests and faces were turned skywards.

The hoofbeats of the unshod Indian ponies faded from earshot and then the stillness of the mountain morning was disturbed only by the praying of the people: their words of worship reaching Steele as no more than a murmuring sound.

He went back to where the gelding was waiting, unhitched the reins from the clump of brush and swung up into the saddle. Rode the horse along a zig-zag course to get clear of the timber and then directly down the open slope.

The priest and his congregation were still at prayer: all but one of them with eyes tightly closed. The exception was John, who was startled by the sight of the lone rider emerging from the trees. And for a moment he seemed set to spring erect and shout a warning to the others. But then the impulse was suppressed and he remained down on his knees. No longer voicing the responses to the prayer which the priest led: tacitly watching the slow progress of the rider on the slope.

Then he lost sight of him, as Steele rode the gelding down into the rocky hollow from which the Paiutes had sprung their ambush.

'. . . it is the will of God that my daughter has been taken from us,' the priest was intoning as the Virginian came close enough to hear plainly what was being said.

'Amen to that,' all but one of the congregation responded.

'We ask that it may be His will that she is returned to us soon.'

'Amen to that.'

'His will be done.'

'Yea, His will be done.'

'Amen.'

'Amen.'

Steele was up out of the hollow and through the rocks as the prayer came to an end. And was seen by more than just John as the people unclasped their hands, opened their eyes and turned their faces away from the sun bright sky: got to their feet.

Mild surprise was the strongest expression on any face at sight of him: this overlaying the heeltaps of terror or the melancholy that showed dully in their eyes.

Then the priest became aware of this new centre of attention as he rose arthritically to his feet. And turned to peer shortsightedly at the newcomer as Steele reined in his mount and touched the brim of his hat with a gloved index finger.

'Welcome, stranger. You are among friends for as long as you wish.'

'Grateful to you, but me and the horse rested enough up in the timber.'

'How long was you up there, mister?' John demanded.

'Hush, son,' a man urged.

This as the priest snapped his head around to direct a chastising glower at the angry young man.

'Saw most of what happened with you people and the Indians,' Steele answered.

John directed a grimace of contempt at the mounted man, which made his handsome face briefly ugly. He was about twenty five. Six feet tall and skinny. With a head of blond hair that was a mass of tight curls. He had bright blue eyes and an angular nose. The thin line of a blond moustache above his wide mouth.

'I ask that you forgive John Boyd his lack of manners, stranger,' the priest said. 'I fear he has much to learn of the principles by which we Aaronites conduct our lives.'

He was also six feet tall, but the stoop of age did not allow him to stretch to his full height anymore. He had lived at least seventy years and the slack skin that hung in folds on the bone structure of his thin face seemed to be inscribed with a line for every day of his life. His eyes were as black as his clerical garb. He had no teeth between his thin lips.

'Did you eat while you were resting, stranger?' the priest went on. 'If you did not you are welcome to join us for a meal.' He glanced up toward the sun. 'It is almost midday.'

The invitation apparently included an instruction, for the women broke from the group to go toward their wagons – one of them trailed by two boys of about twelve.

'Grateful to you,' the Virginian replied and swung down from his saddle. This as the pins were removed and the tailgates were dropped on five of the six wagons.

Now that Wilma had gone, there were six women in the group. Seven men and the two young boys. Less than half of them seemed as pleased as the priest that Steele had accepted the invitation.

'I am Aaron Curtain,' the priest said, extending his right hand. His clasp was firm, his fingers skeletal. When he released the Virginian's hand he gestured with his arm as he reeled off the names of his followers.

The middle-aged couple from the second wagon in the line were Bradley and Grace Horan. Amy and Clinton Rycott were the parents of Tommy and Joel who rode in the third wagon. The young couple were Conrad and Sibyl Grange. Paul and Gertrude Mayne shared their wagon with Gertrude's elderly unmarried sister, Irene Boucher. And John Boyd's parents were Agnes and Hank.

Steele received just a fleeting impression of each of them, noted that some nodded to him and others pointedly avoided meeting his gaze as he acknowledged the introductions.

'Adam Steele,' he said when Curtain was through.

'The padre forgot somebody,' John Boyd growled. 'That was his daughter Wilma the Indians took.'

The young man received another glowering look from Curtain, who then beckoned for Steele to follow him. 'Come, sir. I will prepare a meal for us.'

The Virginian went with the old man to the head of the train, and hitched the gelding to a wheelrim on the shade side of the wagon. While the other men went to join their respective wives who had taken from the supplies the makings of a cold meal.

'If we had made any attempt to prevent the Indians taking Wilma, we would all have been slaughtered, Mr Steele. And my daughter would not have been saved from her fate.'

The horse was hitched to the front wheel of the wagon. The Virginian had sat on the ground to lean his back against the rear wheel as Curtain dropped the wagon tailgate – not speaking until he handed his guest a tin plate on which there was a hunk of sourdough bread and a piece of hard cheese.

'That's the way I saw it from up in the timber, feller.'

Curtain half sat on the lazy board that jutted from the side of the wagon between the two wheels. His slack-skinned, crinkled face was as impassive as that of Steele.

'The first principle of the faith I founded is non-violence, sir. The second demands that my followers share whatever they possess with others who are in need. The reason we have left our Pennsylvania homes to come west is that we may find isolation – where the weakest of us will have the time and opportunity to build a strong foundation for our faith. Before the floodgates open and we will have to constantly put it to the test as we did back there.'

He waved a hand toward the east.

'Reckon you just took the toughest test yet,' Steele said.

Curtain squeezed his eyes tightly closed and sucked in a breath through his toothless gums. 'It was God's will, sir. And I will give thanks for ever that I and my daughter did not flinch. And that the rest of my followers stumbled but did not fall.' He opened his eyes and there was pride in them. 'Even the hot-headed John Boyd was persuaded to keep the faith by my dear girl.'

'Wasn't just his youth that set him off?'

A shake of the head. 'John and Wilma will be wed when she reaches the age of twenty-one. I cannot condone what he did, but I can understand it.'

The Virginian did not have much to eat. Aaron Curtain even less. The old man finished it and set aside his empty plate. Clasped his hands and tilted his face skywards to offer a post-meal thanksgiving for the food.

Along the string of wagons, others finished their frugal meals and gave thanks to their God.

Steele chewed and swallowed a final mouthful and rose to go to his horse. Drank from a canteen to wash down the food.

'Perhaps the Indians will spare Wilma from degradation, sir,' the old man said morosely. 'They are poor wretches who were in need of food. We gave them this and they demanded liquor. But Aaronites have forsworn alcohol. It was in anger that the Indians made Wilma their prisoner. Without alcohol to stoke their lust, perhaps when their anger cools they will repent their actions. Be uplifted by the example of friendship we showed.'

His words were spoken in a tone of hope. But when his dark eyes briefly met those of the Virginian, they expressed a question in such a way that they pleaded for reassurance: and in the same moment showed hopelessness.

Steele unhitched the gelding from the wheelrim and swung up astride the saddle. 'It's not true that the only good Indian is a dead one, Mr Curtain,' he said evenly. 'But I reckon the bunch that took your daughter are the kind that got their nation a bad name.'

The old man suffered overtly for a moment more, then sighed and intoned: 'It is God's will. May He go with you, sir. And may you find a time and a place where there is no need for you to bear arms.'

'Grateful to you.'

Before he turned his horse to ride out along the valley trail to the west, he glanced back along the string of stalled wagons. Where all the Aaronites had now finished their meal and were making preparations to leave. Just John Boyd interrupted his chore to gaze fixedly at the departing rider. Over too great a distance for the Virginian to see if there was aggression or pleading in the young man's bright blue eyes.

'No thanks are required, sir,' Aaron Curtain assured. 'It is our duty to share what little we have. And to offer spiritual guidance to those who have strayed from the path of righteousness. To pray for those who consider themselves beyond redemption.'

Steele acknowledged this with a curt nod and started the gelding forward. Was some twenty feet beyond the lead horses of the front wagon team when John Boyd shrieked:

'For God's sake, mister, help my Wilma!'

The Virginian snapped his head around and was in time to see the beefily-built Hank Boyd fell his son with a single blow to the side of the jaw. So that the boy was unconscious on his feet and became limp, to corkscrew into a heap.

Steele halted his mount and said loudly enough for the old man to hear: 'Seems somebody just broke your first principle, feller.'

'It does not apply to we converts provided it takes the form of punishment, sir. And it is a cardinal sin for any of us to ask help of mortal man.'

Curtain was shocked by the young man's outburst, but unmoved by the vicious punch that silenced him. Then suddenly shocked again as he stooped to pick up Steele's plate from the ground and heard a metallic clink: saw the twenty cents the Virginian had left among the crumbs of bread.

'I said it is our duty to share –'

'My first principle is to pay my way, feller,' the mounted man cut in. 'Because I can't abide to be in debt.'

'You will forever be in debt, sir! To your Creator for giving you life, the Lord God.'

'You could be right,' Steele allowed as he restarted the gelding. And added softly to himself: 'But in my case it always seems there's the devil to pay.'

CHAPTER THREE

THERE HAD been good reason, to his mind, for Adam Steele to accept the old man's invitation to lunch. For in the time it took him to eat the meal, the band of Paiutes could be far advanced to wherever they were heading. Which could be a permanent encampment or simply a suitable piece of terrain, come upon by chance or used on other occasions, where they could rest up: eat the freely given food and enjoy the white woman who had been so easy to take prisoner.

Of course, he could have killed the time alone, eating without payment from his own supplies in the privacy of the timber. But the events he had witnessed at a distance had intrigued him and since it was patently obvious there was no risk in satisfying his curiosity, he did just this.

Now alone again, the string of wagons out of sight behind him and the clear-to-see sign of the Paiutes' passing on the trail ahead, he made no attempt to examine his feelings about the odd Aaronite sect. Instead, concentrated his attention upon the tracks of the Indian ponies and the country that flanked the trail which wound up out of the valley in front of him.

Aware that White Fox and his braves might not travel too far before calling a halt. Their pouches had been filled to capacity with food and they had obviously taken the most sexually attractive woman from the Aaronites. But the supplies would not last forever and it was likely they could tire of Wilma Curtain's body. Sibyl Grange was not much over twenty and she had a pretty face and a fine figure. And the Conestogas were obviously well stocked with food. So White Fox would be a fool, unworthy of being the leader of the band, if he did not stay within striking distance of the wagon train's route. Ready to take advantage at least one more time of the easiest pickings of his life.

So the Virginian kept careful watch for the first clue that he was drawing close to where the Paiutes were camped, poised behind an outer shell of nonchalance to react instantly if he was spotted by the Indians before he saw them. And they attacked him for his horse and saddle, his clothing and weapons, ammunition and food. Hopeful, probably, of finding a bottle of liquor in his saddlebags.

He rode up out of the valley and down into another one that angled north of west, the sign on the little-used trail showing that the Paiutes had travelled the same way in front of him: the tracks no fresher or older than when he first began to follow them.

This new valley was broader than the one behind him, with the pines growing much closer to either side of what he knew was an army trail. But he did not consider angling the gelding into the timber and the cover it provided. For he had spent the best part of two days traversing the forest that cloaked the undulating hills to the south. Often having to veer far to the sides and sometimes to backtrack until he found this trail which an old timer furtrapper had told him cut an easy path through the Big Belt Mountains: at least as far as Fort St James.

And for as long as the sign showed on the trail, he had no intention of leaving it. But it was reassuring to have the timber so close at hand, in the event that the Paiutes did spring an ambush.

He was almost constantly on an upgrade, the trail dipping infrequently into a hollow or along a valley bottom ravine: but invariably the climb out the other end was steeper and higher. And he knew that altitude as much as the lateness of the day was responsible for the chillness of the air. Immediately overhead the sky remained clear and an even blue and the sun that cast long shadows was as bright as ever. But ahead, between breaks in the tree covered ridge he was riding toward, he could see higher peaks. Above the tree line: bare rock and great wedges of year-round snow, with grey cloud hovering over them.

He took from his bedroll a kneelength sheepskin coat and put it on: fastening all but the lowest button and turning up the collar so that it brushed the underside of his hat brim. His breath and that of the gelding began to vaporise as the yellow glare went out of the sun and its light shaded toward crimson.

He rode up out of a ravine and reined in his mount: as he saw a column of smoke that was not as white as the distant snow nor as grey as the cloud above the far off peaks. It showed above the treetops about a mile to the south-west which was the direction in which the trail curved – running level for half this distance before it dipped into another hollow, took a zig-zag course up out of the valley and through a pass over the timbered ridge.

The fire was only recently lit, the column of wood-smoke reaching higher into the evening sky as Steele watched: not disintegrating until it was caught by a current of air that curled down from the pass.

He heeled his horse forward and remained in the saddle until he was on the rim of the hollow. From where he could see that the campfire was burning some fifty yards off the trail to the left, completely enclosed by trees.

He could smell the smoke now, but could not hear the crackle of burning wood nor voices. Down from the saddle, he drew the Colt Hartford from the boot and as he canted it to his left shoulder he thumbed back the hammer. Then he led the horse into the trees on the right of the trail, his free hand on the bridle: his footfalls and the clop of hooves muted by the carpet of pine needles. His hearing was attuned to pick up the first sound to indicate that there was a sentry posted on this side of the trail. But there was no such sound.

Instead, he heard the crack and roar of flames consuming pine wood. Then a voice speaking a language he did not understand – but could identify as the same tongue he had heard spoken by White Fox at the wagon train ambush. Followed by a burst of raucous laughter.

He was directly across the trail from the camp now and so there was no need to check that the sign made by the Paiutes took a turn into the timber at this point – if he had ever doubted it was the Indians who were resting up here.

'You may shame me by defiling my body but you have not captured my soul. My place in the kingdom of heaven is assured. By your actions you have doomed yourselves to eternal purgatory.'

Wilma Curtain was afraid, but doing her utmost to

conceal it. There was just a mild shrillness in her voice and only a slight quiver in the odd word.

One brave laughed in response to her claim, then spoke in his own language. The others laughed.

Steele came to a halt and the gelding snorted softly: the sound masked by the laughter.

'I tell my people what you say, girl. You hear what they think of it?'

'Yes, I heard.' Hopelessness sounded behind defiance.

'You sure you do not wish to eat some of the food?'

The smell of cooking was mixed in with that of woodsmoke now.

'My stomach would reject it.'

'What does that mean, girl?' White Fox seemed genuinely interested – eager to learn.

'I would throw up.'

'I am glad you tell me this, girl. I and my people cannot afford to waste what we have.'

'Which was given with pleasure. For it is much more blessed to give than to receive. Even in the face of such ingratitude as you showed. I would ask that you have your meal now. And allow me a period of peace in which I may pray for the strength of faith to withstand –'

'Do as you want, girl!' White Fox cut in with a flare of anger. 'And pray for me and my people! The whole Indian nation! Those who submit to the demands of the white invaders of their lands! And those who will fight to the death against the invaders!'

One of the braves who did not speak English asked a question. And White Fox interrupted him, too. In the same tone of bitter anger.

Then there were just the sounds of the fire to disturb the stillness of the camp. And Adam Steele made to move on: experienced a stab of ice-cold self-anger at an involuntary impulse to remain where he was.

In the timber above the stalled string of wagons, when he approached the group of whites after the Indians left, while he shared a meal with Aaron Curtain and during the slow ride through afternoon and into evening he was resolutely determined to avoid involving himself in the dangerous trouble that was no concern of his. And until this moment, he had not doubted his resolve to swing around the Paiute encampment and go on his way: needing nothing he did not already possess.

Now, after hearing the terror all but concealed behind the religious fervour of the captive girl, he knew that if he did turn his back on her he would be lacking something of vital importance. Peace of mind.

For stretched seconds, that part of his mind which had been so firmly resolved to stay clear of this trouble did battle with what little conscience that was left to him after so many years of harsh experience and deprivation. And when the good beat the bad, he was able to subdue the self-anger and feel no resentment.

In truth, he felt nothing. The decision was made and now he had to apply himself to dealing with the ramifications – how to set Wilma Curtain free from the Paiutes without getting himself killed or, worse, captured.

He hitched the reins to a low-hanging tree branch and opened a saddlebag: took out a carton of shells and emptied them into a pocket of the sheepskin coat.

The fire crackled and the smell of cooking food became more appetising by the moment. There was low-voiced talk in the Paiute language. Nocturnal creatures made scurrying noises in the forest. Solid night fell on the mountains and the moon failed to penetrate the foliage of the close-growing trees. But it did light up the forty feet width of the trail and its untimbered shoulders.

The Virginian crossed the open strip with long, silent strides some hundred yards beyond the Indian camp. He advanced fifty yards into the timber and then turned to cover about the same distance back toward the Paiutes who were now relishing the hot food. He was reasonably sure no sentries had been posted but was prepared to be wrong so trod as silently as he could and remained tensely watchful.

Fifty yards or so from the camp, unable to see the glow of the fire, he paused, went down on to all fours and in the near pitch darkness felt for dead twigs and old pine cones. Stacked these into a foot-high heap and with two matches was able to set them alight.

Taking as his signal the first words spoken by White Fox since his put-down of the girl before the meal started.

'Now, white squaw! You will do whatever is demanded of you or it will go bad for you. We are Paiutes. Not like our brothers of the Apache, the Comanche and the Sioux tribes. We wish to pleasure ourselves with you, but not to harm you. But if you do not do everything asked of you, it will be an insult to us. And we Paiutes are a proud nation.'

The second match transferred its flame to a piece of very dry twig just as the leader of the braves finished the warning. And there followed a sound of ripping fabric accompanied by a gasp from the captive girl.

His face impassive in the flickering light of the embryo fire, Steele rose and walked quickly out on to the trail. Throaty calls of encouragement to their leader from the braves masked the Virginian's heavier footfalls as he moved with greater speed. On to the trail and back along it, then into the trees to the east of the camp. Where he slowed to angle toward the place where Wilma Curtain was pleading:

'I do not wish to be harmed. I will do as you ask. But I have no experience of this. No man has ever . . . please be patient –'

White Fox cut across what she was saying with a burst of excited talk in his own language. And what he said was greeted with a roar of approval. Steele guessed the lust of the braves was heightened by their leader's revelation that the girl was a virgin.

He went down on to all fours again and crawled to the fringe of a clearing some sixty feet across. A semi-permanent campsite for the band of Paiutes for there was a large cooking pot on the fire at the centre. Four wickiups in an arc on the far side. A rope and pole corral on this side in which the ponies were confined.

The animals were weary from the day's travel and for the most part were unmoving: so that Steele could look under their bellies and between their legs and see the component parts of the camp scene clearly in the light of the fire which was supplemented by the glow of the moon.

All ten Paiutes were there, nine of them standing in a loose group to the left of the fire, watching what White Fox was doing to the girl.

The leader of the band was down on his haunches, using a knife to cut the underthings off her body now that her plain dress, ripped from neckline to hem, was spread beneath her.

She lay utterly still as her nakedness was revealed to the lusting eyes of the Indians. On her back, her wrists lashed together and held out above her head, tied to a short stake driven into the ground. A slim girl who her father had told Steele was not yet twenty-one. With short, head-hugging chestnut hair. Her face immaturely pretty. The bones of her ribcage showing clearly through her sparse flesh below the mounds of her breasts, flattened by her supine position. Her belly very flat with a bushy triangle of dark hair at the base and the top of her slim, pressed-together thighs.

White Fox sheathed the knife and was gentle in the way he drew off her boots which left her totally nude. When she allowed pent up breath to whistle from her slightly parted lips which now moved a little in the mouthing of a prayer.

One of the standing braves said something and all of them laughed.

White Fox growled huskily: 'Ocheo is perhaps the dullest brained of my braves, girl. But he just made joke. Says that if you always are so when you are on your back, it is to be expected that no man has ever taken you.'

He was still squatting at her feet after easing off her boots. Now gripped an ankle in each hand and pushed them to either side, splaying the legs of Wilma Curtain.

The watching braves divided into two groups, the better to see the fully exposed sex of the girl as White Fox came erect and began to unfasten his weapons belt.

Steele shifted his impassive, unblinking gaze away from this prelude to mass rape: to peer beyond the cooking pot on the dying fire and between two of the wickiups – seeking a glow to indicate that the new fire was taking hold in the timber to the west. But if it was, the intervening trees hid it. He returned his attention to White Fox and drew a bead on the side of the Indian's head with the Colt Hartford: lying in the classic prone position for a rifleman – elbows resting firmly on the ground to keep the weapon steady.

'Is there . . . nothing I . . . can say to stop you doing this?' the girl pleaded.

Her faith no longer acted to shield her from the terrible reality of her situation. There was dread in her voice and tears trickled from the corners of her eyes to run down into her hair.

'When a woman is presenting herself as you are to a man as I am, nothing can stop what must happen.'

He allowed his buckskin trousers to fall around his ankles: to expose his rampant lust.

The girl had raised her head from between her upper arms to peer at his face as she made her plea. And felt compelled to shift her gaze when he looked down at himself.

'Dear God, don't let this man hurt me!' she wailed as her head fell back.

And White Fox dropped to his knees between her splayed legs.

Steele tracked his head target downwards, squeezing his gloved index finger tighter to the trigger.

But the exploding bullet did not blast out of the muzzle of the Colt Hartford. And White Fox was uninjured as he fell to the side and rolled out from the vee of the girl's naked legs when he was just inches from penetrating her.

This as the other Paiutes whirled and crouched, clawing for the revolvers on their weapons belts. Snapping their heads around to stare between the wickiups, into the timber from which the shot had come. Giving vocal vent to their shock as they saw the glow of a large blaze in the trees. Then hurling themselves to the ground as a volley of exploding shots followed the initial crack.

Adam Steele gave a soft grunt of satisfaction that some – maybe all – of the shells he had placed in the hastily built fire had exploded with the heat. A little late, but not too late.

White Fox began to shriek orders at the braves as he reached for his trousers and scrambled to get them on. And the braves raced to comply with his commands – lunging into the wickiups and emerging with their Winchesters.

Wilma Curtain was shrieking shrill words, most of them incomprehensible. Except that the name of God featured often. Then she was silenced as White Fox snatched up his weapons belt, released the revolver from it and struck her a hard blow with the butt against her temple.

Two more bullets were exploded by the heat, cracking out sharply against the dull roar of flames taking a hold on living pine trees.

The Paiutes were still in a state of high panic: unable to rationalise that no bullet had cracked into the clearing. Were certain only that all the shots had sounded in a single direction. And followed White Fox's orders to counter attack against the unseen enemy.

So they raced between and around the wickiups, firing blindly on the run. And White Fox sprinted in their wake as soon as he had buckled his belt around his waist.

Steele was up on his feet and ready by then. Ducked under the rope and zig-zagged among the protesting ponies as soon as the leader of the Paiutes went between two of the wickiups. Then ducked under the rope on the far side of the corral: gaze constantly raking from the way ahead to the area where the Indians went from sight.

There was a constant barrage of gunfire now and he

knew he had a better than even chance for as long as the shots continued to crack out. Unless White Fox suddenly suspected a diversionary trick and in the wake of panic became cool-headed and backtracked with some of the braves.

Steele reached the naked girl: and rather than waste time drawing the knife from his boot sheath and cutting her free, yanked out the foot length of stake that was sunk into the ground. Saved more time by not raising her from the ground. Instead, dragged her across it with just one hand fisted around the stake where the rope was tied. She on her back and he taking long backward strides, so that he was able to keep his eyes and the Colt Hartford directed across the campsite at the wickiups and firelit timber behind them.

He took the shortest route across the open ground of the clearing and hauled his burden into cover on the south side. Not needing to negotiate the ropes of the corral and the milling ponies. And a dangerously long way from where his own horse was hitched: and from the wide trail that would act as a firebreak against the flames he could hear raging in this area of pine forest.

Ten feet back from the fringe of the clearing, he had cut the rope holding her to the stake but not that around her wrists when he heard anger vented in a foreign tongue.

Muttered to the unhearing girl: 'Reckon I got nobody but myself to blame that it's the bloodlust has a hold of them now.'

CHAPTER FOUR

HE LEFT her where she lay on the forest floor and moved from one tree trunk to the next until he was able to crouch behind some brush and survey the clearing.

The braves had evidently spread out wide to follow the initial order yelled by White Fox. For just the leader and six others had run back into the camp area.

The absence of the girl was spotted immediately and after his enraged reaction to this, White Fox was now snarling commands at two of the braves while the other four raked their eyes and the muzzles of their Winchesters over three sides of the clearing. Fear rather than anger was dominant on their dark-skinned faces as they sought a sign of Wilma Curtain's rescuer.

The two braves White Fox was yelling at nodded their heads and swung around to race back between the wickiups. Sent to round up the trio of Paiutes who were still blasting bullets to useless effect west of the camp.

And the leader of the band was calmer now, reason prevailing over rage as the sounds and smells and glow of the forest fire came relentlessly closer. He snapped more orders and after a few moments of anxious hesitation, the four braves allowed that he was right.

Which was when Steele showed a brief smile and backed away from his vantage point to return to the naked girl. For the Indians abandoned their fearful watch on the dark arc of trees: tacitly acknowledging that the roaring fire to the west was a more imminent danger than whoever had taken their prisoner. And they hurried to dismantle the wickiups and gather up the scattered gear that littered the campsite. To saddle the ponies and load their equipment on to travoises. Working frenetically to move what little they possessed out of the path of the leaping flames.

The Virginian saw only the first few moments of hectic activity in the clearing before he withdrew. And took the time now to cut the girl's wrists bonds and to drape her light weight over a shoulder before he swung through the timber to arc around the east side of the clearing.

Smoke was like tendrils of mist in the air, but not yet thick enough in this area to impair vision or dry the throat. But the burning trees to the west gave off a glow that dulled the light of the moon.

The grey gelding was still hitched to the tree bough, but was skittish from the stink of fire assaulting his nostrils. And the animal snorted with heightened fear at the approach of Steele with the nude Wilma Curtain draped over his shoulder.

The Virginian spoke soft, soothing words to the horse and within a few moments his voice was recognised. And he was allowed to get close enough to stroke the nose with a gloved hand. The gelding's nostrils remained flared to the acrid taint of drifting smoke, but his eyes ceased to bulge.

The unconscious girl was transferred from the man's shoulder to the saddle of the horse. Then the man unhitched the reins and tugged gently on them: to turn the horse and lead him without haste back eastwards. Along the fringe of the trees at the side of the trail. To the mouth of the ravine from which he had first spotted the smoke of the Paiute's fire.

There was a brush-covered crag to the south of the trail here and he had to lead the gelding halfway around it before he found a way to get the animal halfway to the top and into a position from which he could watch the country to the west. And in the time it took to reach this new vantage point, he merely glanced back at the burning forest every now and then.

But once he, the horse and his unconscious charge were in cover, he devoted most of his attention to watching for the Indians.

The fire was raging as fiercely as ever, the roar of the leaping flames occasionally punctuated by the crash of a falling tree. Oily black smoke seemed to blot out the sky above this entire region of the Rockies. There was no break in the timber that he could see to the south of the trail and he had a short-lived image of many hundreds of square miles of pine forest reduced to a charred wasteland. All to save the honour of a young girl he did not even know – he could not be sure that her life as well as her virginity had been on the line.

He glanced down at where she lay among the rocks on the hollowed-out ledge which arced around the south-western curve of the crag. And saw she was still breathing. But still unconscious. It had been too long for the blow from the revolver butt to be entirely responsible and he guessed it was shock that continued to keep her under.

Her naked flesh was goose-bumped and tinged with blue and he took off his sheepskin coat and wrapped it around her. She remained utterly limp and made no involuntary sound of protest when he moved her.

He looked at the sky again and saw he had been wrong about the smoke. Certainly it was a thick blanket in the immediate area of the blazing timber, but elsewhere it was low, dark cloud that cloaked the mountains.

A snowfall or rainstorm was promised by the low cloud ceiling: and as a native of Virginia, born and bred amid lush, green countryside, Adam Steele experienced a brief hope that the weather would close in soon to minimise the fire damage to the forest – and a stab of fear that high winds might precede the downpour.

But then his concern with the fire and the weather was abandoned. For he saw movement on the trail where it came up out of the hollow in which the Paiute camp had been sited. Saw what he had half expected to witness when he took up his position on the face of the crag.

White Fox's band had all survived the flames and seemed to have saved everything they owned. For Steele counted all ten braves astride ponies, six of the mounts dragging travoises which were equally laden.

Instinctively, the Virginian thumbed back the hammer of the Colt Hartford when he first saw the Indians. But he did not bring it to the aim through the vee of rocks from which he was watching.

Unlike the slow-riding Paiutes, who sat rigidly tense

in their saddles: Winchesters clear of the boots. Rifle muzzles constantly tracking back and forth across the timber flanking the trail.

White Fox rode at the head, his braves formed into a short column of threes behind him.

Steele pursed his lips and allowed air to hiss softly out between them. The need for killing had been a strong possibility ever since his conscience demanded he help the girl. Now it came closer with each stride of the Indian ponies.

The non-violence principle of the Aaronites had played no part in the Virginian's act of freeing Wilma Curtain. It was simply that he was not prepared to force a shoot-out with a ten to one disadvantage. But events were now shaping to bring about a show-down – because White Fox had every reason to believe that the non-violent Aaronites were responsible for stealing back his prisoner. And he was not prepared to call it quits. He had been defeated by a trick and was not about to turn his back on this and endure humiliation in the eyes of his braves. Not when the enemy was a group of whites who did not even carry arms.

Which meant that by rescuing the girl, Adam Steele had committed himself to protecting the entire group of religious fanatics from being massacred – something he had determined not to do when he first saw the Paiutes making a headlong charge upon the whites that morning.

The Indians were in no rush now. They moved just fast enough to stay ahead of the forest fire: and to keep careful watch on their surroundings in case the whites had another trick ready to spring. This while, somewhere to the east, the Aaronites were encamped for the night: maybe worrying about the suffering of the girl as they prayed for her, and ignorant of the danger that threatened them.

Below the crag at the mouth of the ravine, White Fox revealed that he had not simply been watching the fringes of trees for the unexpected: that his Indian eyes were seeing sign. For he raised a hand to signal the braves to halt their mounts at precisely the point where Steele had led the gelding away from the side of the trail to find a way up on to the crag.

Now the Virginian lifted his rifle from where it leaned against his knee and thrust it out through the vee in the rocks. Saw a large bead of moisture explode on the barrel. At the same moment as another hit the front of his hat brim and splashed down on to one of his gloved hands.

White Fox tilted back his head to peer up at the face of the crag, faintly illuminated by the fringe glow of the fire.

Adam Steele squeezed the trigger of the Colt Hartford. And the leader of the Paiute band saw the stab of the muzzle blast. But the bullet travelled faster than he was able to move and it tunnelled into his chest at the instant his muscles made to obey the command from his brain. So that it was the impact of the lead rather than a voluntary physical move that pitched him sideways off his pony.

The brave immediately behind White Fox also took a bullet in the heart while the whole band was staring with stunned shock at the falling body of their leader.

A flurry of rain spattered the mountains.

Adam Steele thumbed back the rifle's hammer and tracked the barrel to the left. Aligned the sights on a brave who was aiming a Winchester up at the crag. Squeezed the trigger a third time as he saw the muzzle flash from the Indian's weapon. Ducked his head low as chips of rock sprayed with greater intensity than the rain drops. Stayed low and cocked the Colt Hartford again as a whole volley of shots sounded and a hail of rock splinters flew. And voices were raised in shock and anger and fear.

The rain beat down harder and he became aware of the icy feel of the drops against his flesh. Was also aware that if the weather developed into a heavy storm, it would be to the advantage of the Paiutes. For there were still seven of them down there who might be prepared to separate, leaving their horses while they advanced up the crag on every side under cover of teeming rain. Moving in on a man encumbered with an unconscious girl.

The fusillade lasted for several seconds. During which Steele bellied along the indented ledge. Now peered from around a rock ten feet to the right. Saw that three of the braves were crouching beside the gunshot ones, checking for signs of life, while the other four aimed their rifles up at the crag: two still astride their ponies and the others down on the trail.

The rain was falling hard and fast but he could still see the scene on the trail clearly in the light of the fire which had not been noticeably diminished by the precipitation. He could have perhaps shot two more braves before the others zeroed in their rifles on his new position. But he held his fire and by touch ejected the three spent shellcases from the cylinder of the rifle and reloaded the chambers: without shifting his gaze from the Indians.

The three braves hit by Steele's bullets were apparently dead. And since White Fox was one of the corpses, the survivors seemed undecided about who should give the orders now. Then one of them emerged as a temporary leader and the others complied with his commands: he and two more continuing to cover the crag with their Winchesters while the others made preparations to withdraw. First draped the corpses over their respective ponies, took up the reins as lead lines and got mounted themselves. All the time casting anxious glances up at the crag from which death had struck. Then the watching trio swung into their saddles and the ponies were wheeled around. To head back west, with travoises or corpse-burdened animals hauled behind.

They were out of sight before they rode down into the hollow, lost behind the curtain of rain that was now heavy enough to be having an effect on the fire. Drenching the flames so that hissing steam was mixed in with the smoke.

Once he could no longer see the Paiutes, Steele moved back to where the girl lay and his gelding stood. He draped her, still wrapped in the sheepskin coat, over the saddle again, and began to lead the horse down the crag by the same route he came up it.

The ground was slippery and he mouthed many silent curses as he divided his attention between keeping the gelding calm, preventing the girl from sliding out of the saddle and watching for a sign that the withdrawal of the Indians had been just a ploy.

The teeming rain which penetrated his clothing and struck icy to his skin, in combination with the retreat of light as the forest fire was extinguished, brought almost pitch darkness to the mountain night.

But he made certain that he returned over his own backtracks and thus had a bearing on the trail when he reached level ground.

And was sure he was almost at the mouth of the ravine when Wilma Curtain vented a high-pitched scream of terror: flailed her arms and legs when he reached out to hold her in position, and pitched head-first off the far side of the horse. Naked again, for he was left gripping the empty, rain sodden coat.

'Quiet, lady!' he rasped as he jerked the horse to a halt and swung around the animal's tossing head. Saw her pale body spread-eagled on the muddy ground: mouth still gaped wide to power out the scream that had an eerie quality in the storm-lashed night.

Then the sight of him, just an indistinct figure looming over her, acted to constrict her throat and trap the sound inside it. Her eyes snapped wide now, perhaps as she was hit by total recall of what was about to happen to her before she was clubbed into unconsciousness.

But her hands were now free. 'No,' she managed to force out as she covered her face with her clawed fingers, then wrenched herself over on to her belly.

Steele eyed impassively the length of her back and her slim buttocks above the slender columns of her thighs. And growled: 'Reckon your Pa would be proud of you, lady. Way you've done what the Good Book says and turned the other cheek.'

CHAPTER FIVE

WILMA CURTAIN began to sob, but she did not struggle when the Virginian had to half drag her to her feet. She just shivered violently, kept her face covered with her hands and seemed to be oblivious to the present while her anguished mind recalled the recent past.

He draped the coat over her shoulders and fastened two buttons. She gave him no help at all in getting astride the saddle but once on the horse she sat rigidly enough to avoid sliding off. Her sobbing diminished, but she continued to tremble and he guessed this was more a symptom of shock than of the biting cold.

If the Paiutes had made a strategic withdrawal as a prelude to a surprise attack, they were not close enough for her piercing scream to reach them and bring them running.

Steele led the gelding out on to the trail as the rain became streaked with sleet, reducing visibility to a few feet.

The girl's lower legs, not covered by the coat, were blotched with blue patches and he knew she would suffer badly from exposure unless he got her into shelter of some sort soon. Was aware, too, that he was in the same danger. And he chose to combat this known threat to the exclusion of concern with the possibility of the Indians closing in.

So he concentrated entirely on keeping on the trail down into the ravine and glanced over his shoulder only to check that the girl remained in the saddle.

A wind was driving the sleet now, coming from the north, so at the low point in the ravine he angled off the trail to the north wall. The icy drops of moisture were eddied and swirled at the base of the rock face, but visibility was a little better.

He was halfway up the gentler slope toward the eastern end of the ravine when he saw an almost vertical cleft in the rock. Twenty feet high and maybe two and a half wide. How deeply it cut into the wall he could not tell – just that it narrowed rapidly.

He halted the gelding beside the crack and yelled to the girl: 'Get down off of there now!'

She continued to sit in the saddle like she was already frozen, hands still masking her face. Did not respond when he slapped her thigh. So that he had to slide each of her bare feet from the stirrups, drag her out of the saddle and keep her from collapsing when she was on the ground. The only sound she vented was a small gasp.

He experienced an anger as icy cold as the night as he wrenched one of her hands away from her face and slapped her hard across the exposed cheek. She gasped louder now and looked at him with hurt rather than pain.

'I have things to do, lady!' he snarled. 'You can't stand up on your own feet, you fall on your bare ass!'

He released her and she staggered to the side: would have fallen had she not banged into the rump of the horse. The animal sidled away from her with a snort and she swayed, but remained erect.

And Steele went to work quickly. First took the saddle off the gelding, turned it upside down and pushed it into the bottom of the cleft. Then he unfurled the bedroll, ignoring the cooking and eating utensils which were scattered over the muddy ground. Draped one blanket around the compliant, uncomprehending girl and another over himself. Then bundled her into the crack, sideways and standing on the more or less dry underside of the saddle. Forced himself inside, facing her so that they were pressed against each other at thigh, belly and breast. The Colt Hartford he jammed in back of him between his rump and the rock. The oilskin rain slicker which had been on top of the bedroll he draped over their heads like an unribbed umbrella.

Thus, although they were both bitterly cold from the soaking they had already received, they did not get any wetter and the girl's bare feet were not sunk into mud. While the reasonably dry blankets served to keep in the natural body heat that began to become re-established.

Outside the crack, the gelding's animal instincts drew him close to the base of the rock wall, out from under the full driving force of the sleet.

There was no talk for a very long time while they stood pressed intimately together, he standing a little less than a head taller than she so that his jaw was on a level with her brow. She continued to shake for several minutes and occasionally her teeth chattered. While he constantly raised and lowered each foot in turn, clenched and unclenched his gloved fists and flexed the muscles of his arms and shoulders: head turned to the side so that he was looking out into the ravine.

Maybe if White Fox had still been leading the Paiutes, they would be hunting for the girl and her rescuer despite the storm. The Indian's determination to make the whites pay for shaming him overriding every other consideration. The Virginian thought it less likely the seven survivors of the band would give revenge precedence over the need to seek shelter. But he had not survived countless other brushes with death by failing to take account of all the possibilities: so now he took steps to guard against the pain of cramps and the danger of stiffened joints hampering his actions should the Paiutes stumble on to the hiding place.

'Who are you?' the girl asked huskily.

He turned his head away from the ever-moving veil of dirty white sleet which blotted out everything more than ten feet away. To look down into her face: in the darkness of the cleft under the draped oilskin could see just the whites of her eyes and her teeth against the paler colouration of her thin face.

'A fool called Adam Steele, Miss Curtain,' he growled.

The whites of her eyes were briefly obscured when she blinked several times and he now realised she was no longer trembling.

'Just you?'

He returned his gaze to the restricted view beyond the cleft in the rock. 'Reckon not. The world is full of fools. You were travelling with a whole bunch of them.'

'There was shooting as the Indians were about to . . .' She swallowed hard and shuddered. Then made a choking sound, like it was bile she was trying to force back down and almost failed. 'Then he hit me. I don't recall anything else. I had nightmares, I think. Or perhaps they were not?'

'It doesn't matter. You were stripped naked and hit on the jaw with a gun butt. You got very wet from the storm. Nothing else happened to you.'

'I will thank God for that.'

'Whatever you want.'

'And you may demand of me whatever I am able to give, Mr Adam Steele. My faith does not allow me to ask help of mortal man. But if it is given without request, an Aaronite is obligated to discharge the debt.'

'Your Pa told me a few of the Aaronite principles.'

She caught her breath in a sound of shock. 'My father did not ask you to –'

'No, miss. Your beau did, and got a crack on the jaw from his Pa for it.'

She sighed. 'John requires much tutorage before he will be fully converted.'

Steele made no response and the girl remained silent for a long time. The sleet continued to drive hard down into the ravine and the Virginian kept up his restricted exercise programme.

Then: 'It was John who told you about the Indians taking me, Mr Steele?'

'No, I saw what happened. Your Pa invited me to lunch – like he was repaying me for not interfering.'

'He will be indebted to you for saving me.'

'He doesn't owe me a thing.'

She continued as if there had been no interruption from him. 'Unless you resorted to violence to set me free?'

She was tense with expectation of the worst.

'I killed three of the Paiutes, lady.'

The shudder that shook her body this time was unrelated to the cold of the mountain night. And he felt her try to draw back from him in the confined space as a further mark of revulsion.

'I would rather be dishonoured a thousand times than have anybody harmed to prevent it.'

'It was my life on the line, too,' he replied in the same growling tone he had used throughout the exchange. 'And I'm not an Aaronite.'

'Not even a Christian?' There was spirit and strength in her voice for the first time as she made the accusation.

'Born and brought up a Calvinist, lady. Last time I recall being in a church, I had to kill a man.'

She gasped. 'Had to?'

'It was in the war. But I reckon I was a lapsed Calvinist before then.'

'You have no belief in the Creator?'

Steele directed a globule of saliva out into the night. 'Reckon something had to create all this, Miss Curtain. But it didn't take as long as six days to get it started. And a few million years to grow into what it is. And we make our own heaven and hell the way we live our lives.'

Because he was not looking at her, he thought he had shocked her into silence. But she was merely reflecting sadly on his philosophy. And after a few seconds, delivered her verdict.

'You admitted to being a fool, and that is what you are, Mr Steele.'

Now he did glance down at her upturned face, and drew back his lips to show a gentle smile that, if the light were better, she would have seen acted to drop several years from the burnished, lined face. 'Why else on a night like this would I be wedged into a hole in a rock with a near-naked girl – passing the time with a theological discussion? When there's a chance that seven mad-as-hell Paiutes who want my life and your body will come and find us?'

She was not touched by his humour, and neither did his mention of the Indians reawake dread. It was repugnance that showed in her face and sounded in her voice when she answered: 'From the way you keep moving against me, Mr Steele, it would seem that you are stirred by lust for my body!'

The Virginian held the smile in place. 'You said I'm entitled to ask for whatever you're able to give, lady. And since right here and now you've got nothing but yourself . . . ?'

He allowed the unfinished sentence to transmit the obvious implication. Expected her to shudder again and maybe to give vocal outlet to her feelings. But instead she became utterly rigid, snapped her eyes tightly closed and said evenly:

'If that is what you want, take it.'

His smile became instantly transmuted into a tacit snarl. And as his body set as inflexibly as her own, she opened her eyes: drew in her breath at sight of the anger on his face.

It took him a second longer to bring the impulsive anger under control. His voice was colder than the night.

'I keep moving so that my circulation doesn't slow down, lady. I don't want to get the cramps and if I need to move fast I want my muscles to do what's asked of them when it's asked. And right now the last thing I can think of asking them to do is screw you.' He turned his head to spit again. Added: 'No offence intended.'

'I'm sorry,' she said meekly after a pause. 'It's hard for me –'

'No, lady,' he cut in. 'I'm cold as ice, soaked to the skin and standing up. Even if you were my type, it wouldn't be hard for you.'

CHAPTER SIX

IT WAS more than an hour later before the storm began to slacken and during this time there was no further talk between Adam Steele and Wilma Curtain. They shared their body heat and the girl managed to wriggle in such a way that the blanket draping her head and shoulders dropped down to protect her exposed legs beneath the coat.

The Indians stayed away.

When the wind blew itself out and visibility through the sleet turning to rain lengthened to several yards, the Virginian said:

'Wake up, Miss Curtain. Time to go.'

For a long time she had been limp, her forehead resting on his shoulder and seemingly kept from falling only by the way she was wedged so tightly between him and the rock at her back. But she responded immediately to what he said, bringing up her head to show that her eyes were brightly devoid of any sign of sleep.

'I haven't been sleeping, Mr Steele. Praying to God.'

'There was time and I reckon it can be done anywhere. But now we have to move. Maybe you can get through to Him again when we're riding.'

'Your mockery lacks conviction, Mr Steele.'

'And your religious fervour is getting to be a trial, Miss Curtain. When I slide out of here, you could feel like you don't have a leg to stand on.'

He reached down to grasp the Colt Hartford and squeezed out into the drizzle. The rain slicker completely enveloped her head and muted her cry of alarm when her legs gave way and she fell forward.

The sad looking gelding snorted and then stood in pleasurable submission as the Virginian used a blanket to rub him down as the rain finally stopped. But cloud still blotted out the moon and stars.

The girl came tentatively out from the cleft, the blanket and oilskin bundled in her arms, the sheepskin coat still draped over her shoulders. She vented a squeal when she stepped off the underside of the saddle and into the ice cold mud.

'Be grateful if you keep the noise down,' Steele told her. 'With the storm over, the Paiutes could be on the move, too.'

'I'm sorry.'

She watched him dolefully as he cinched the saddle to the back of the horse and made a pouch of the oilskin, stowed his cooking and eating utensils in this and tied it to the horn. Then, with the blanket wet from rubbing down the horse draped over his shoulders, he swung astride the saddle. And looked across at her.

'Suggest you wrap that blanket around you like a skirt, Miss Curtain. With the opening at the front so it'll keep your rear and your legs warm while you ride.'

She took his advice and moved toward the horse

when he extended a hand and freed his left foot from the stirrup. It was awkward for her to get astride the cantle with Steele gripping one of her hands while she clasped the makeshift skirt to her waist with the other. Then to arrange herself so that the blanket encased her rump and legs. And she made certain that the coat, with her arms in its sleeves now, and the blanket draped from Steele's shoulders, intervened between her belly and his back before she announced she was ready.

He heeled the horse forward, out on to the trail and eastwards up the gentle slope. After a few yards, she was compelled to reach her arms around his waist and clasp her hands at the front.

'Pray all you want, lady,' he allowed. 'But I'd appreciate it if you'd keep your eyes and ears open. And tell me ahead of God if you see any sign of the Paiutes.'

'I have offered Him my thanks and asked that he forgive you and the Indians, Mr Steele. It is not yet the time for morning prayer.'

The Virginian responded with a noncommittal grunt and they rode in verbal silence for perhaps a mile, he keeping the horse to an easy pace despite the animal's eagerness for speed and the warmth this would generate.

By this time, the vaguely rancid smell of sodden burnt timber was left behind.

Then the girl said: 'I do not think you are a fool, Mr Steele. Although it cannot be denied it was extremely foolhardy what you did – there were ten of them and just you alone.'

'I know it.'

'It will go hard for John if you let it be known to the Aaronites that you answered his plea to help me.'

'I didn't.'

'You didn't?' She was surprised.

He pursed his lips and vented a soft sigh. 'The Paiutes took you the way I intended to ride, Miss Curtain. Spent most of yesterday afternoon searching for them to ride around them.'

'But you didn't?'

'I didn't.'

'Couldn't?'

'I said you were getting to be something of a trial, Miss Curtain. But that doesn't mean you can cross-examine me.'

'I'm sorry. It's just that I'm interested in your motives. I find it difficult to understand a man like you.'

'Maybe that's because you've led such a sheltered life.'

She made an affirmative sound. 'There can be no denying that, Mr Steele. My father founded the Aaronite sect several years before I was born. And since he was the founder, I have been required to adhere more strictly to the faith than anyone else. Except for the padre himself, of course.'

'It didn't catch on, uh?'

'I'm sorry?'

'Counted sixteen on the wagon train before you left. Including two kids not old enough to be sure of anything.'

'Oh. Yes. No, there are more, Mr Steele. Over a hundred. Back in Altoona Pennsylvania and the country around there. But we have been hounded and belittled, abused and persecuted ever since the padre began to preach the principles of the Aaronite faith. Every Aaronite wished to join in the journey to a place where we will be free to live and worship according to the principles and not be harassed and abused for our beliefs.

'But we are all poor people and when we pooled everything that could be spared, there was only enough to purchase and supply the six wagons. When we have found a place to settle we will let it be known to the other followers of the padre. And they will come to join us as soon as they are able.'

'You have a piece of country in mind?' Steele asked.

'No. We will travel until God makes it known to us that we have reached the place.'

'Hope for your Pa's sake that's before you get to the ocean, lady.'

'It is in the hands of God, Mr Steele.'

'He gave Moses a helping hand, but I reckon the Pacific is a different proposition to the Red Sea.'

'After the scorn we have endured for so many years, your brand of ridicule does not hurt us.' She sounded very proud.

'Isn't there anything in your Pa's principles to suggest that maybe God has a sense of humour, lady?'

'We laugh a great deal, Mr Steele. When the circumstances are conducive to it. Now, if you will excuse me, I must attend to morning devotions.'

The sky on the horizon ahead of them was shading from black to grey as the false dawn began to break.

'You're excused, Miss Curtain,' he answered. 'But you don't have to say one for me. I've heard tell that the closest a man can get to heaven is to have the company of a silent woman.'

She appeared not to hear him, suddenly withdrawn into a private world of her faith. And he did not intrude as the true dawn came and the cloud in the east took on a crimson tinge from the rising sun.

He devoted his entire attention to maintaining a survey of the mountainscape on all sides and did not swing his head around far enough to more than glimpse her serenely composed face when he glanced over his shoulders.

The sun was up, but showed as just a pale yellow disc behind the cloud when he saw the line of wagons far to the east. Parked on the sloping trail that led down into this valley from the narrower one that stretched in a direct east to west direction beyond the crest.

There were no signs of life in the vicinity of the halted train and Steele was visited by a few moments of concern – that the Paiutes had ridden through the ravine unseen or had gone east by another route, to hit the unsuspecting Aaronites under cover of the storm in the dead of night.

But a few minutes later, when the doubly burdened gelding was moving up from a hollow which hid the head of the valley, he saw smoke. And when he was in a position to see the distant wagons, there was movement around them.

Six cooking fires caused the smoke to column upwards, attended by the women. While men were bringing the teams off a patch of good grazing in the forest, to hitch them to the Conestogas.

'When you're through, lady, you can see your people from here.'

'I can see them now,' the girl replied at once, in a melancholy tone.

'And the circumstances aren't conducive to happiness?'

'I am worried that you will not be believed, Mr Steele. That Mr and Mrs Boyd will not accept you did not act because of what John asked.'

The Virginian grunted, then spat to the trail. 'I told you the kid got smacked in the mouth for talking out of turn. What other kind of punishment is allowed? Can he be branded on the forehead with a T for traitor? Or could he be in line to get hung, drawn and quartered?'

'He can be banished from the faith,' she answered grimly. 'In which event he will be driven away not merely from the Aaronite community but his family. And he is not like you, Mr Steele. He could not survive alone in this kind of country.'

'From what I saw when the Paiutes sprang the ambush yesterday, he'll have as good a chance on his own as with –'

'Please do all you can to convince them that John did not influence you, Mr Steele,' she cut in fervently.

'And not spill the beans about you asking me to help him, lady?'

'I love him! In ten months we are promised to be married.'

'I'll tell it like it happened. And warn them they're likely to get more trouble from the Paiutes. Which is the reason I've taken the trouble to bring you all the way back to them. Since it was me stirred up the Indians. What they do about what I tell them is up to them.'

'I cannot expect more from you than this, Mr Steele,' she answered with resignation.

And there was silence between them again as they closed with the line of wagons which were being got ready to leave as soon as breakfast was through. But the Virginian did not need to hear Wilma Curtain speak to be aware of the tension that took a tauter hold on her as the distance to the wagons grew less: could feel it in the way she gripped him around the waist and the rigid attitude of her body pressing against him.

The meal was finished, thanks had been given for the food and the fires were out when the horse and its two riders were seen by one of the Aaronites. Who brought it to the attention of the others.

'They look as happy to see you as you are to be back,' Steele growled as the final chores before leaving were abandoned and the people gathered into a close-knit group beside the team of Aaron Curtain's lead wagon.

Perhaps there was talk among the waiting people, but there was no excitement in their stance: no animated gestures of greeting.

'I think I gave you ample warning not to expect a hero's welcome, Mr Steele.'

'I didn't mention me, lady. Just you and them.'

They rode over the final few yards of trail and he reined in the gelding immediately in front of the group of silent, grim-faced men, women and boys – the father and fiancé of the safely returned girl as stoically devoid of joy as everyone else. The forbidding expressions clear to see on freshly shaved and scrubbed faces.

The emaciated, stoop-shouldered leader of the group broke the silence as soon as the horse was still.

'We are obviously indebted to you, sir. If you will tell us how we may repay you, we will endeavour to meet your requirements.'

Adam Steele felt an ice-cold ball of anger in the pit of his stomach which he knew threatened to expand and turn white hot – the churlish attitude of the Aaronites made the more inappropriate because they were freshly rested, cleaned up and fed while he and the girl were none of these things. And he had to make a conscious effort to remain impassive and keep his tone of voice even.

'Any of these wagons carrying a bath-tub, feller?'

'All of them, Mr Steele. Cleanliness has a close proximity to Godliness.'

'Relight a couple of fires and heat enough water for two tubs. Cook some breakfast on the side. With coffee.'

If not seen or heard, the Virginian's anger was sensed by certain of the Aaronites whose dogged grimness cracked to reveal discomfiture. Aaron Curtain was not among these.

'We were about to continue on our journey, Mr Steele.'

The Virginian sensed the girl was having to struggle against a threat of trembling.

'You reckon you owe me something, feller. It was your idea. I can live with being tired, dirty and hungry for awhile longer if you can't pay off this debt you think you're in. But unless your daughter has been excommunicated or whatever, helping her off my horse won't hold you up for too long.'

There was a stretched second of silence as the cold, coal-black eyes of Steele looked out from his bristled, mud-streaked face to rake over the group. And he saw that at least half the Aaronites were anxious to speak, but dared not to say anything that might conflict with the padre, who had his back to them. Until the sixty-year-old, frumpish looking spinster named Irene Boucher blurted:

'An hour or so will be neither here nor there, padre.'

Those who agreed with her were relieved that she had the courage to speak their minds. John Boyd was among these. While those who considered the word of Curtain was immutable law directed severe looks at her.

The white haired old man visibly flinched at the interruption. Then announced: 'It is my decision that it is the will of God that you be offered what you require, sir. Bradley and Conrad, attend to the comforts. Agnes and Gertrude, kindly help my daughter to dismount. The two children will take care of the needs of your horse if you wish it, sir?'

'Be grateful, feller,' Steele replied as Mrs Mayne and Mrs Boyd came po-faced to help down the girl while Bradley Horan and Conrad Grange set about their designated chores with a will. And the Rycott boys were held back by their scowling mother, who seemed reluctant to have them go near the Virginian.

'As are we to have Wilma back with us, Mr Steele,' Curtain said.

The girl was as stiff from the ride as she had been after taking shelter in the ravine: would have fallen had the two women not helped her out of the saddle and supported her when she was on the ground. The blanket fell from around her waist and there were gasps and grimaces as imaginations were sparked by the sight of her bare legs below the sheepskin coat.

John Boyd seemed on the verge of tears and at the point of lunging toward her. But was forced to remain where he was when his stern-faced father hooked a meaty hand over his shoulder.

Tommy and Joel Rycott approached hesitantly after Steele swung down from the saddle.

'A rub down and some feed will be fine, kids,' he told them as he handed over the reins. He showed the youngsters a brief smile, then was impassive again when he looked at Aaron Curtain. 'Don't want to stay too long where I'm not welcome.'

The entire group broke up now, leaving Steele and

Curtain in isolation beside the team in the traces of the lead wagon.

'You are not an Aaronite nor are you God, sir. You have helped one of my followers after being requested so to do. Which breaks one of the principles of our faith.'

'What the Boyd kid asked didn't –'

'Hear me out, sir! And in view of the circumstances we fear that in bringing my daughter back to us, you resorted to violence. Thus broke our first principle and perhaps even one of God's Commandments. As Christians, we will fulfil the commitment you have specified. But are more anxious than you are that the time of our parting should come soon.'

He swung around and strode to the rear of his wagon. Climbed up into it. Said something in a severe tone which caused Gertrude Mayne and Agnes Boyd to emerge from the Conestoga, relief showing on their faces.

Wilma Curtain began to talk in low tones to her father.

John Boyd growled something to his father that spread rage across the face of the older man. Then the lanky youngster with the head of tightly curled blond hair came across to where Steele was picking up the blanket which had fallen away from Wilma.

'Mister?'

The Virginian straightened wearily, both blankets slung over his shoulder. 'Yeah?'

'Did them Indians . . . did they do anything to her?'

'Stripped her and scared her, feller. That's all.'

He looked weak with relief. Chewed the inside of his cheek for a moment. 'In the night, before the storm, we saw a big fire over to the west.'

Two fires were already lit on the ashes of earlier

ones beside the line of wagons. And the pots for the baths and the cooking were in place. Horan and Grange left their wives to fix the meal and coffee and moved up behind John Boyd. Irene Boucher joined the group and this encouraged Clinton Rycott to move in the same direction.

Resentment was the dominant emotion with which they were eyed.

'I needed a diversion,' Steele said.

'But it wasn't enough, mister?'

'To get her away from the Paiutes, yeah.'

'But then?'

'They came after us, feller.'

'And found you?'

'Maybe they would have done anyway.'

'Maybe?'

'It looked like White Fox spotted our sign. But the rain started about then and would have washed out our tracks pretty fast. Way it happened, I shot White Fox and two of his braves before –'

'Dear God!' Irene Boucher gasped, and dropped to her knees, hands clasped and face upturned toward the low clouds.

Grange, Horan and Rycott took their cue from the spinster as everyone else looked with horror toward the scene beside the team of the lead wagon. Where only Steele and John Boyd remained standing.

The younger man swallowed hard and gazed out along the valley to the west. 'Just three, mister? There are seven still alive?'

'There's nothing wrong with your subtraction, feller. And I reckon you can work out what it could add up to?'

'They'll cause us more trouble.'

Steele spat to the side and growled: 'Some.'

CHAPTER SEVEN

THE VIRGINIAN took his hot bath in the Horan wagon, immediately behind the Curtains' Conestoga in which Wilma scrubbed off the physical effects of her ordeal. The balding, fleshy-faced and solidly built Bradley Horan brought Steele a plate of salt bacon and grits and a tin mug of coffee just as he finished shaving off the last of the bristles on his jaw.

'Prayer meeting over?'

It was while Steele was stripping off his clothing to get into the wooden tub on the bed of the cluttered wagon that he heard Aaron Curtain call his followers into a congregation. Then listened to the old man as he communed with God in a toneless voice. First gave thanks for the safe return of Wilma with her virginity intact. Next asked that the Paiutes and Steele be forgiven – the Indians for their lust and the Virginian for laying waste an area of the Lord's creation and for taking the lives of three of his children. Then pleaded that the souls of White Fox and the other dead braves be admitted to heaven. And finally requested that the

Aaronites be granted a peaceful continuation of their journey to wherever God was leading.

He dressed up his invocations with a great deal of rhetoric and Steele's hunger took on a finer edge as the appetising aromas from the cooking and coffee pots wafted into the heavily laden wagon.

'Sure is, mister,' Horan answered. 'And if you've a mind to pour scorn over the way us folks run our lives, it'll be like water off a duck's back. Don't figure you know any insults we ain't had to take in the past.'

Steele accepted the plate and mug that were thrust toward him and shook his head. 'Firm believer that every man should be free to worship how he pleases, feller. But now you people are through with spiritual matters, I reckon you ought to do something about –'

'Figure young John is fixin' to take that on himself, mister,' Horan cut in morosely.

'No, Pa!' John Boyd yelled defiantly. 'It has to be said! And I'm not the only one here who knows it! Listen to me, all of you!'

'I'm sorry, padre,' the youngster's father pleaded.

'I know, Hank,' Aaron Curtain assured him ruefully, as Horan hurried to climb down from the wagon and a woman began to cry. 'Hush, Agnes. Take strength from your faith. Whatever is to be will be.'

Expectancy seemed to have a palpable presence in the stretched seconds of silence.

'I can't talk the same way as the padre,' John Boyd said suddenly as Steele began to eat his breakfast. 'I don't have the words. And I ain't claimin' to be smarter than him in anythin'. But I got to say that I think we'll be fools if we keep headin' along this trail the way we are!'

'What do you suggest, John?' Curtain asked in a patronising tone. 'That we turn back? What purpose would that serve? From what Wilma has told me, the Indians who survived the unwarranted attack by the murderous stranger who is amongst us did not have sight of him. They must therefore assume he is one of us and that we lied when we said we did not bear arms. So we must assume they will seek vengeance. On horseback they can quickly overhaul us and will surely see our retreat as an admission of guilt.'

'I'm not sayin' we oughta go back, padre,' John Boyd said vehemently.

'Good, John. To remain here would be pointless and because of the terrain and our mode of transport we cannot deviate from the trail. Therefore, we must press on just as we intended before the stranger and Wilma returned. Without stealth or connivance. So that if the Indians are bent on avenging their dead, they will be encouraged to talk with us instead of attacking us. Allow us the time to explain that the stranger acted on his own initiative. In direct defiance of what he was told.' He paused and Steele could visualise him gazing fixedly into the face of the rebellious youngster. Then: 'Is there anything else you wish to add, John? Or are we in complete agreement?'

'You can only guess at what the Indians will do, padre.'

'As can you, John. But whatever comes to pass, we have to believe it is the will of God. If we do not, then –'

'Father, White Fox is dead!' Wilma Curtain called from the rear of the lead wagon.

'Everyone is fully aware of that, child,' her father countered impatiently.

Steele was out of the tub now and towelling himself dry.

'So how will you be able to explain anything to the

Indians?' she said bitterly. 'He was the only one of them who knew English.'

This reminder drew a surge of anxious talk from the Aaronites. Which John Boyd cut across by voicing the idea that had obviously been at the back of his mind when he opened the discussion.

'That's right! But even if it wasn't, I don't trust them Indians to do like the padre figures! So I think we oughta have protection! I think we oughta ask Mr Steele to ride with us and –'

'John!' Hank Boyd thundered.

'No, Hank!' Conrad Grange cut in. 'Let the boy be! Or punish me, too! On account of he's said what I've been thinkin'.'

'I'm sorry, padre, but so do I,' Clinton Rycott added. 'I can see Amy don't agree with me, but I ain't ready to risk the lives of our two boys who ain't near old enough to make up their own minds in circumstances like this.'

Steele dressed slowly, taking a regular sip from the mug of coffee.

There was a babble of agreement and disagreement with John Boyd's plan. And this time it was the leader of the group who silenced it.

'A basic principle is questioned by more than an individual follower!' he announced in a funereal tone. 'I therefore call a convocation. From which I propose that my daughter and John Boyd be excluded. In addition to the Rycott children, of course.'

There was a chorus of 'Amen, padre.'

Then the shuffling of feet as most of the group moved along the line of wagons.

Amy Rycott called: 'Joel, Tommy, attend to putting out the fires and cleaning the dishes and pots. And empty the tubs.'

Thoughtfully drinking the last of the coffee, Steele watched the group trudging toward the rear of the final wagon in the train. None of them looked into the Horan wagon.

The more spotty-faced of the two Rycott boys appeared as the Virginian lowered himself to the ground, fully dressed and with the collar of the sheep-skin coat turned up against the chill of the overcast morning.

'We done like you asked with the horse, sir.'

'Grateful to you. You're not allowed to take payment?'

'No, sir. Sir?'

'Uh?'

'You said your name was Adam Steele, sir. But there's a plate on the stock of your rifle says it was given to Benjamin Steele by Abraham Lincoln.'

'Ben was my Pa, kid.'

'It's a fine gun, sir. And Mr Lincoln was a fine man.'

'Two of the best, I reckon.'

'Mr Steele!' John Boyd called.

'I hope you ride with us, sir,' the boy said eagerly. 'Maybe have time to tell Joel and me about the gun and Mr Lincoln?'

The Virginian did not reply as he swung around the rear of the wagon and went to where the anxiously frowning John Boyd stood beside Wilma behind the lead Conestoga.

'John is concerned you will be angry that he spoke as he did without asking you first, Mr Steele,' the girl said in a tone and with an expression that was protective toward him.

She was wearing an identical dress to the one White Fox had ripped off her – grey and loose fitting so that it guarded her modesty and kept her warm but did nothing to stress her girlhood on the brink of womanly sexuality. The kind of dress all the Aaronite females wore in the manner of a uniform. Now that her face was freshly scrubbed the bruise on her jaw from the blow with the gun butt showed ugly purple under her pale skin.

'That should be the least of his worries, shouldn't it?' the Virginian countered with a gesture of his head toward the gathering at the rear of the train.

Wilma shook her head. 'He ran a grave risk in questioning one of the basic principles without being sure others would support him. But whichever way the vote goes, John and those who agreed with him cannot be punished. And if there is a majority in favour of what he suggests, then he can hardly be banished for your actions last night.'

'Reckon not, lady.'

'And if you are asked, mister?' John wanted to know anxiously.

'He'll do it,' Wilma put in before Steele could reply. 'Because it's the absolute truth that nothing you or anybody else said made him act in the way he did last night. His conscience made him do what he did, out of plain and simple humanity. And he has to do so again. It's even more important to him this time. Because if the Indians were to attack us, it would be his fault. And he could not endure to have such a massacre of innocent people troubling him for the rest of his life.'

She looked hard into the Virginian's impassive face as she spoke: as if she were not so confident as she sounded and searched for a tacit sign that she was right.

'They say that in a tub of hot water is the best place to think,' Steele said evenly.

'And did I think it out correctly?'

'Maybe. Did you have the time to figure what I'd do if the vote goes the other way?'

'I think you'll think of something.'

She showed him a knowing look that verged on a smile. Which left John Boyd totally puzzled.

Then there was movement among the people at the rear of the wagon train, and the meeting broke up. The men and women came toward the trio at the front, the group diminishing as the various Aaronites left it to climb aboard their respective Conestogas. Nobody looked triumphant or defeated.

'You have been given everything for which you asked, sir?' Aaron Curtain asked without enmity.

'No complaints, feller.'

'That is good.' The clop of hooves sounded and Steele looked along the line of wagons to where Joel Rycott was leading his horse forward. 'We are to continue our journey now. You are most welcome to accompany us and share what is ours. But on one condition. You must set aside your arms.'

John Boyd squeezed his eyes closed and compressed his lips in a momentary display of emotion. But then became as resigned as everyone else to the result of the meeting.

'Grateful to you, kid,' the Virginian told Joel as he took the reins of the gelding from the boy, who turned and ran back to the wagon of his parents. John Boyd went in the same direction with less haste, as Steele swung up astride the horse.

'As we are to you, sir. For your attempts to protect and help us. But it is our fervent hope that you will never again try to impose your violent ways upon the Aaronite faith which is diametrically opposed to meeting force with force.'

Just for a moment there was a flare of anger in the

shortsighted eyes of the old man as he peered up at the mounted Virginian. Or perhaps it was a burning hatred for the stranger who had caused his authority to be questioned by his previously blindly faithful followers.

Steele nodded to the priest and touched his hat brim in the direction of the girl as she gave him another knowing look: but this time with no suggestion of a smile in back of it.

'Luck to you people.'

He heeled the gelding forward.

'A vacuous wish, sir,' Aaron Curtain called after him. 'We would rather you prayed for us. As we will remember you at our devotions.'

'Be a waste of whatever time you people have left, feller,' he told the Curtain father and daughter as he rode alongside their wagon. 'Reckon I'm too deep in hock ever to be redeemed.'

CHAPTER EIGHT

HE DIDN'T push the gelding back along the valley but even so the distance between himself and the crawling line of Conestogas lengthened by the moment. And within thirty minutes he could no longer see the wagon train when he looked back.

He rode the familiar stretch of trail in the same cautious way as yesterday and the early hours of this morning: watchful for sign of the Paiutes' presence. Knowing the Indians would not mark their position with a fire now.

The mountain air remained cold and the dull, low clouds continued to threaten another downpour. But the weather was still dry at noon when he rode up out of the ravine in which he and the girl had sheltered from the previous night's storm.

He could see the tract of burnt timber from here and smell the taint of old fire. Saw that maybe a couple of acres of pine trees had been totally destroyed, with a fringe band to the west, south and east which had suffered to a lesser extent. The trail had acted as a break to prevent the flames spreading northwards. The clearing in which the Paiutes had been camped showed as a lighter coloured patch off centre of the expanse of sooty blackness featured with areas of grey ash.

Through the pass in the ridge to which the valley trail led, he could not see the snow-capped mountains beyond. For the weather had already closed in on the higher ground.

A little way beyond the area of destroyed timber he was able to see sign of the Paiutes' ponies and travoises in the mud that thinly coated the trail. The sign commencing at the point where the Indians had sheltered from the storm among a scattering of boulders. And where, after the storm was blown out, they had buried their three dead in a communal grave – then marked the resting place of White Fox and the other two braves with a mound of small pieces of rock.

Steele rested his horse here, and ate some jerked beef washed down with canteen water. Heard an unfamiliar clinking sound in one of his saddlebags and delved into it to find the cause. Discovered that the twenty cents he paid Aaron Curtain for yesterday's lunch had been returned to him.

He remounted and continued up the sloping, zigzagging trail toward the pass. And did not rein the gelding to a halt as he rode by the place where the Indians' tracks angled into the timber to the north: a half mile in a direct line from the gap in the ridge.

His face was impassive as he sat easy in the saddle on the slow-moving horse: revealing nothing of the inner struggle that occupied his mind. But there was really no contest on this occasion – and no spark of self-anger as he reflected on the inevitable.

There was no pathetically helpless girl denied divine

intervention to spur his actions now. But no external influences were necessary, since his decision had been made before he rode on ahead of the wagon train. And in the way she directed those knowing looks at him, the girl who was not then in danger and helpless had shown she was aware of his decision. Which had irritated him more than a little as he rode through the cold, dull morning. Resentful – because it was in his nature – that someone knew him well enough to predict what he would do on such short acquaintance.

Now he was eager to fulfil her prediction. Unburden himself of the responsibility for stirring up the Paiutes against the Aaronites. And be on his own, unfettered way again. The whole crazy business behind him.

So he rode the gelding all the way up to the pass in an apparent attitude of easy nonchalance: his posture offering no clue to the fact that he was tensed for trouble and poised to react to it. Just as he had been during the entire ride: even though he thought there was a better than even chance the Indians would rather ignore than tangle with him.

For they had their sights set upon a bigger prize than one lone-riding white man. Instead, a whole bunch of them, with women. Who must be made to pay for the lives of three braves. And whose wagons, horses and supplies would provide a bonus in the wake of the vengeance raid.

So, Steele had reasoned, the Paiutes would prefer to let him pass unhindered rather than risk the sound of gunfire alerting the people on the wagons to trouble ahead. But he did not entirely trust his assumption and thus did not feel as relaxed as he looked until he was at the pass and out of sight of watching eyes on the slope. Where he dismounted and slid the Colt Hartford from the boot as an integral part of the move.

He had no doubt at all that the Paiutes were below him: waiting and watching for the wagons of the Aaronites to start up the zig-zagging trail toward the pass. For it was a perfect ambush point, with no space to turn the rigs and the up grade too steep for the teams to haul the heavy Conestogas at any speed. For there was no other reason for the Indians to leave the trail and strike into the dense forest where the going for the travois-dragging ponies was much harder.

Beyond the pass, the horizon was drawn closer by the bad weather sweeping down from the snow-covered peaks to the west. But for as far as he could see, the terrain spread away in the form of a high plain: wooded to the south but mostly bare rock elsewhere. An inhospitable piece of country, bad to be caught in by a storm as fierce as that raging around the distant high ground.

But if the bad weather did spread eastwards and the Aaronites chose to keep rolling through it, their fate was not his concern.

He hitched the gelding to a branch and moved silently away from the animal after taking a carton of shells from a saddlebag. He went back the way he had come, but stayed in the cover of the timber which grew on both sides of the pass.

There was a vast area of forest on the north side of the head of the valley and the Paiutes could be anywhere in it. But he worked on the assumption that they would not be too far off the trail: close enough to take up ambush positions in good time when a sentry signalled that the wagon train was approaching.

So the Virginian remained on a course parallel with the trail and only some thirty feet into the timber. Carried the rifle canted to his left shoulder and uncocked until he guessed he was nearing the place where the Paiutes had angled off the trail. When he thumbed back the hammer and brought the gun down to his side: left gloved hand fisted around the frame.

The sweat of tension broke out on his forehead and his head began to buzz with the strain of listening for a sound alien to those of his own progress. And the muscles of his legs suddenly ached from the unnatural gait which was necessary to mute the noise of his advance.

He heard a sound and froze – one foot in the air at the start of another stride. Even held his breath. Recognised the sound as that of a man spitting. Ahead and to the right. No more than a few yards away.

He tracked the rifle in that direction and set down his foot. Opened his mouth wide to guard against the expelled breath whistling through his teeth.

He had been moving along a natural path through the forest, going toward an elongated clump of thick brush some four feet high. The man who had spat was on the other side of the brush. Not standing up, or else Steele would have been able to see him.

The white man did not move a muscle while he waited for the Indian to make another sound: expected this time, so that he could get a precise bearing on the Paiute's position.

And perhaps two minutes later, the brave unwittingly obliged. He broke wind.

Ahead and to the right – and at higher than ground level. Maybe ten feet higher.

Steele tilted the rifle in his left hand and moved toward his objective, blinking sweat beads off his eyelashes. Was at the side of the brush when he saw the Paiute. Straddling the branch of a tree, his legs interlocked beneath it. His back to Steele as he peered out along the trail, eastwards from where the tracks of the entire band led into the timber.

And the sweat turned ice cold on the face of the Virginian as he realised how close he had come to death. An Indian had not been perched on the tree branch when he rode past less than an hour ago. But the sentry would not have withdrawn far into the trees to wait for the lone white man to go by. Could have killed him just for the hell of it. Would certainly have done so had Steele revealed his interest in the tracks.

Now, though, their positions were reversed and it was the Paiute who was quite literally a sitting target for the white man over a range of about twenty feet. Perched up there on the branch, his Winchester resting across the bark in front of him, one hand on the stock and the other on the barrel to help keep him balanced.

But the Virginian did not want to use the Colt Hartford unless he had to. So he stooped slightly, to gape the split seam in his right pants leg. Drew the knife from the boot sheath.

A silent kill would not bring the other braves running or, worse, cause them to scatter and stalk him the way he had closed in on this one – but from six different directions.

Twenty feet was too far to guarantee that the spinning knife would find a vital spot and sink in deeply enough to kill the Paiute before he gave vent to pain and fear.

But there was no chance of breaking through the brush without alerting the Indian and his shout of alarm would produce the same result.

Then the sentry unwittingly solved Steele's problem. When he broke wind again and gave a grunt of irritation that it was necessary to come down from the tree. Which he did, after making sure the trail to the east was deserted.

He simply unclasped his legs, swung a leg over the branch and dropped with a natural agility to the ground, the Winchester gripped in one hand. Then he moved around the trunk of the tree and close to the clump of brush.

Steele was down on all fours by then, and crawling to a point on this side of the natural hedge immediately opposite the spot where the brave dropped his pants and went into a squat.

Sound and smell drew the Virginian to the precise position. Where he let the Colt Hartford lie on the ground and slowly unfolded upright. To look down over the three-feet-wide tangle of thorny brush upon the hatless head of the Paiute.

Under other circumstances the brave would probably have sensed impending danger. But he was too occupied with what concerned him to be aware of the threat. Was able only to wrench his head around and gape his mouth wide at the sound of Steele's voluntary fall across the brush. Then the blade of the knife sank into his throat below the Adam's apple. And the only sound that emerged from his wide mouth was a moist gurgle. His eyes recognised death and then became glazed as death claimed him. He went limp and sat down hard in his excreta.

Steele rolled on to his side in the snagging brush and jerked the knife out of the Indian's throat. Blood spurted from the brave's mouth and from the wound to splash on to the gloved hand of his killer.

Then the Virginian turned his head to look at the corpse and wrinkled his nostrils as he growled: 'That's a lousy, stinking way to die, feller.'

He had to struggle against the clinging thorns to get

free of the brush. Where he picked up the Colt Hartford and used it to fend off the snagging creepers as he got to the other side of the brush clump by way of the partial breach he had made when he hurled himself into the lethal attack.

Once through, he wiped the blood off the knife blade on the buckskin jacket of the dead brave before replacing it in the sheath. He also cleaned the back of his right gloved hand in the same manner. Then left the body where it lay, the old Navy Colt still on the weapons belt and the Winchester on the ground nearby. Started to follow the sign again, cocked rifle held in a two-handed grip across his belly.

There were just six Paiutes remaining in the band. The same number of shells in the fully loaded Colt Hartford. And maybe there would be a chance to give the rifle a numerical advantage – if he could get close enough to another lone brave to use the knife or the scarf.

But he didn't count on it as he stalked his prey through the silent forest, breathing air that was still damp from last night's soaking. He didn't count on anything except his skills as a hunter and a killer.

Skills which he had started to learn when little more than a child back in Virginia. Where his father had been one of the wealthiest plantation owners in the state. And hunting for sport had been a regular and enjoyable pastime. Then came the war when men in the blue uniform of the Union replaced game as the prey. And there had been times as Adam Steele rode the eastern battlegrounds as a lieutenant in the Confederate cavalry when he treated the war as sport – made the more enjoyable because the hunted could suddenly become the hunters and the danger was heightened.

In the immediate aftermath of the war's end had come the violent peace. Which left the Steele plantation a burnt out ruin and Ben Steele the victim of a lynch mob in a Washington bar room. And the young soldier returned from the war had no sport at all in riding the vengeance trail to track down and kill the lynchers of his father. Using those skills learned during his youth and honed to perfection by war. Avenging his father's death with the Colt Hartford revolving rifle which was his sole inheritance from an estate which a few years earlier had been worth a fortune. A rifle which, as one of the Rycott boys had noticed, had a gold plate screwed to the stock with the inscription: *To Benjamin P. Steele, with gratitude – Abraham Lincoln.*

The way in which the son made the murderers of the father pay for their crime was ultimate proof that the rift which war had opened between them was healed. But it was, of course, an embittered remedy. Made worse – much worse – because the lawman who came to bring Adam Steele to justice for his wanton slaughter of the lynchers was his best friend. And the former cavalry lieutenant, still reacting to any danger as if the war was not yet over, chose to kill again rather than face capture.

It was likely Adam Steele would have escaped the legal consequences of his vengeance ride. But in killing Deputy Jim Bishop he stepped across a line which would forever bar him from the opportunity to rebuild some semblance of what once had been his. And he rode west, doomed by events to move from one violent episode to another. With few respites and each apparent chance to put down roots in pleasant surroundings turning out to be another prelude to an experience with evil.

It took him a long time to come to terms with such a life – to accept that the pattern of his existence was dictated by his ruling fates. Which were set upon punishing him more severely than man-made laws ever could. And in accepting this, he threw down a challenge to those fates which mapped his destiny – hardened himself against the effects of pain and anguish, deprivation and disappointment: hunger, thirst, discomfort and every other brand of suffering that forced most men to conform. Hoped for nothing good from life but took it in his stride when the unexpected happened.

Unlike the Aaronites, had few principles by which to live his life. Kept his word, paid his debts and returned favour for favour. And – the one that motivated him as he neared the Paiute encampment this overcast afternoon – the need to right any wrong he committed.

And he had been wrong to allow his conscience to steer his actions when he rescued Wilma Curtain from the Indians – without killing the entire bunch instead of just three. Better to have left the girl to her fate in the clearing and for White Fox to decide if the Aaronites should be made to suffer further because of their faith in the Almighty to the exclusion of all else.

For he might well have set the girl free and allowed her and the rest of the whites to pass by without further harassment. But whether he did this, or massacred the whole group of whites, would have been no concern of Adam Steele.

But as it was, Wilma had called it right. The conscience which had caused Steele to free her from the lusting Paiutes would never allow him to rest if he ignored the undisputed fact that his actions had driven the Indians to seek vengeance.

So now he sought to complete the chore of rectifying the error. Moving through the forest as cautiously as when he was searching for the sentry: watching and listening intently. Confident the braves would be taking their ease, dangerously unaware that another of their number was dead.

But then he saw the camp and a bead of sweat squeezed from every pore and became ice cold on his flesh: was hit by the dread that he had misjudged the plans of the Paiutes.

For there was not a brave to be seen at the point where the easy to follow sign ended under a bluff which at this area of the head of the valley presented an insurmountable obstacle against reaching the top.

The ponies were there, confined in a rope corral. And so were the travoises, still laden with supplies and the dismantled wickiups. Brush had been trampled, empty cans and pieces of food wrapping littered the area and the cold ashes of a small fire could be seen.

But where were the Paiutes?

The Virginian's hands fisted tighter around the frame and barrel of the Colt Hartford as he swung it out from his right hip. And wrenched his head from side to side, dark eyes searching for a human form. Every fibre of his being tensed to feel the impact of bullets tearing into him. But there was not a movement or sound from the lichen-stained face of the rugged bluff or the surrounding trees.

And Steele's lips curled back to show an expression that was part sneer and part smile. As a sigh rasped softly out through his clenched teeth.

If the braves were watching him from hiding, they did not plan on killing him quickly with a fusillade of shots. Which gave him the time to recover from the paralysing effects of fear and shock at the unexpected.

And prepare a defence against their more subtle strategy.

But he was wrong again.

Instinctively dropped down on to his haunches and swung his head to look directly at an area where he glimpsed movement out of the corner of an eye. Peered from the cover of a clump of ferns at a thicket of bunchberry and pine saplings spread from the base of the bluff at one side of the corral.

The foliage of the bush and the young trees was trembling in the still, damp air – a regular enough occurrence for the ponies to continue their foraging undisturbed.

And the expression on the Virginian's features became an unadulterated smile when he saw a Paiute belly into sight and get to his feet. Yawning and stretching his arms to the sides: obviously just awakened after a long period of sleep.

The brave looked around him without suspicion and grimaced as he shivered. Not relishing the chill dampness of the outside world after the dry warmth of what had to be a cave in back of the thicket.

He went to one of the travoises and took a drink of water from a canteen. Gargled and spat out the water and whatever bad taste was in his mouth.

Then he came toward Steele's hiding place, heading reluctantly to relieve the sentry who he did not know was no longer perched on the tree branch down at the side of the trail.

The brave wore his weapons belt, but apparently was prepared to take over the rifle from the sentry whose period of duty was over.

Six feet from where the Virginian was hunkered down amid the ferns, the brave veered away and started down the trampled stretch of brush and moss and fungi which connected the trail with the camp. He was still yawning and moving his muscles to rid them of the stiffness from sleep. Totally oblivious to everything outside his own private world of minor discomfort.

Until he heard movement in the ferns behind him to his right. When he came to a sudden halt, was frozen for part of a second, then started to whirl: hand clawing for the Colt on his weapons belt.

But by that time Steele was fully erect and lunging forward. His hands free of the Colt Hartford which lay among the ferns. His left hand streaking away from his neck, fisted around one of the weighted corners of the thuggee scarf. Which began to curl under the momentum of the weight in the opposite corner as Steele's hand flicked from left to right.

The Paiute, half turned to face the danger, had his attention captured by the outstretched arm of the white man: expecting to feel the impact of something heavy. But instead he became aware of the touch of the silken fabric at the side and nape of his neck. Was perplexed and then concerned by the white man's right hand thrusting forward and upward, gloved palm open.

Now the brave, his features contorted by fear, swung his body to face the attacker. And abandoned the move to get his gun. Instead brought up both his hands to claw them around Steele's wrists – which were crossed over at his throat.

But Steele flung his right hand to the left and vice versa, each fisted around a weighted corner of the scarf: to draw tight the oriental weapon of strangulation around the throat of the Indian.

The brave's hands, unable to maintain a grip on the wrists of the Virginian, became talons which tore at the fabric choking him. But it was futile. As was his attempt to drive a knee into the white man's crotch. For the scarf bit deep into his flesh, bulging it to either side. And with one of his feet off the ground, it was simple for Steele to unbalance him and drag him forward.

The white man stooped but did not bend double: so that the Indian's legs and belly were on the ground, but his torso and head were held aloft. His dusky skin turned to purple and his mouth gaped, tongue lolling out over his lower lip. His eyes bulged. The veins in his temples showed up as ridges. He made muted gasping sounds. His hands fell away to flop on the ground. Then his eyes glazed and the lids closed as the lack of oxygen brought on unconsciousness. But Steele maintained the stranglehold with the scarf until his victim passed painlessly from unconsciousness into death. Only then released one corner of the scarf so the Paiute slumped face down on to the forest floor.

He swung around then, to peer at the brush-covered entrance of the cave. Nothing moved there. And he half smiled at a few of the ponies who were eyeing him dolefully.

'Wasn't meant to impress you,' he murmured as he retrieved his rifle and hung the scarf back around his neck. 'Just to take his breath away.'

Steele took deep breaths himself, to recover from the tension and exertion of this new killing. Then moved to complete the self-appointed task of finishing off the whole of White Fox's band: the threat of the bad weather in the west spilling through the pass to hit the valley the main reason why he elected not to play a waiting game.

Instead, took the Colt off the weapons belt of the dead brave and exploded two shots into the air.

Hurled the gun away and moved quickly to the point where the trees ended at the bluff, twenty feet away from the concealed cave entrance. And stood behind a trunk.

The shots erupted snorts and whinnies from the ponies, but he could hear nothing to indicate that the braves in the cave had been disturbed.

Perhaps a half minute later saw the tell-tale trembling of the thicket's foliage which signalled the presence of at least one Indian within the cover. But he stayed his finger on the trigger of the cocked rifle: would have done so even had he known all five braves were out of the cave. For he wanted to be able to see his targets – and be sure he scored hits against vital areas. Prepared to play a waiting game to this extent so that he could guard against the danger of one or more braves playing possum.

The horses calmed and familiar silence clamped down over this area of the forest. The thicket was unmoving again. But for no more than a minute. When there was a violent shaking of leaves and branches and a single Paiute lunged into view. Raced across open ground and flung himself down beside a travois piled high with sections of wickiup. The brave carried a Winchester, the muzzle of which raked over the same sections of terrain as the fear-filled eyes of the Indian.

The cover which the Paiute gained did not hide him from Steele, but still the Colt Hartford remained unfired as the Virginian withdrew his head behind the tree trunk. And now had to rely on his sense of hearing to tell him of the Indians' further responses to the sound of the two shots and the sight of the dead brave.

Softly rasped words in a language he did not understand, the rustling of foliage, the dragging of legs along the ground and the padding of lightly placed footfalls. All this through the buzzing noise of strain which once again rang in his ears.

The volume of the external sounds remained constantly low for what seemed a very long time: although it was probably no more than a minute or two. Then one of the braves raised his voice to speak with the authority of giving an order.

Which Steele took as his signal – an indication that the Paiutes had fallen for his ploy – assumed the killer of the brave had been unaware of the hidden cave and had withdrawn. For why else had they been able to come out into the open without attracting fire?

The Virginian stepped into the gap between the tree and the bluff. Saw four of the braves in a loose group as the fifth broke away to go toward the corpse. All of them still nervous and with their Winchesters held ready to swing toward the first threat of danger.

It was the one ordered to check on the dead brave who first saw Steele. And vented a shrill cry of warning as he tracked his rifle toward the stranger.

Steele shot him in the heart, and ended the life of another brave in the same way before the first one curtailed his scream and thudded to the ground.

The surviving trio were panicked by the sudden burst of violence and fired their rifles instinctively – not taking the time to aim. Any one of the three bullets which cracked in his general direction might have drilled into Steele as he hurled himself to the ground. But two thudded into the tree and one ricochetted off the rock of the bluff. And another Paiute died, blood and pulp flying away from his head as he took the bullet that Steele exploded as he pitched forward.

Then the Virginian's choice of the revolver action of

the Colt Hartford for speed over the greater magazine capacity of the Winchester with the lever action paid off yet again. For he had his rifle cocked as he slammed to the ground while both remaining Paiutes had only half completed the necessary moves to pump fresh rounds into the breeches of their guns.

He blasted at the one who was in a crouch, still facing him with the muzzle of the Winchester moved just a fraction off target by the action of working the lever. Another heart shot that sent the victim sprawling backwards against the travois with a wickiup stacked on it.

The final brave had decided that gaining cover on the far side of the travois had greater priority than getting off another shot at the deadly accurate white man. And with his rifle cocked behind a live round in the breech, he powered into a dive. Venting a yell that might have been of rage, fear or despair. But whatever emotion initiated the cry, agony continued it. For the fifth bullet that cracked from the smoking muzzle of the Colt Hartford went between the splayed legs of the brave and tore through the vulnerable flesh of his genitals.

The Paiute crashed down into cover, but as Steele lunged to his feet, he saw the Winchester of the injured man sail up and clatter to the ground amid the rearing and snorting ponies.

The Virginian raced around the travois and pulled up short. The Indian had ceased screaming now and was curled up into a ball on his side, both his hands reached down and clawed at his blood-gouting wound. He was muttering softly to himself, but then sensed the proximity of the intruder and he wrenched his head around to stare in depthless hatred at him. Began to shriek in his native tongue: spittle spraying from his mouth. Obviously hurling every obscenity he knew at the white man.

'You've probably never said any truer words, feller,' Steele told him evenly and would have preferred it had the brave averted his face as the acrid smelling muzzle of the Colt Hartford was lowered toward it.

But the Paiute continued to stare and snarl at the Virginian until the instant when the final bullet blasted from the rifle drilled a neat entry wound in the centre of his brow.

From a range of just three inches, the lead had the velocity to burst out through the back of the brave's skull. And the power to thud his head back to the ground – to hide the awful mess of blood, tissue and bone splinters that gushed from the exit wound.

The drifting gunsmoke was neutralised by the damp, chill air. And the ponies became quiet again. So that the metallic sounds of Steele ejecting the spent shellcases from the chambers of the rifle's cylinder and reloading the gun rang out very loud.

There was no longer any trace of a smile on his face. The job he felt he had to do was completed satisfactorily: but he experienced no sense of satisfaction.

Now he set about putting the finishing touches to it. He took two ponies from the corral and attached a travois to each of these, allowing the other animals the freedom to leave if they wanted to. He unloaded the travoises and dragged two bodies on to each, draped the other two corpses over the backs of the ponies. Then burdened one travois with the additional weight of six Winchesters.

He led the laden animals down the slope through the timber to the side of the trail where he had killed the sentry and heaped the other dead braves on top of this one. Next made a tripod of three of the Winchesters at the centre of the trail and rested the others against this. Finally freed each pony from his travois and, before starting on foot up to the pass where his gelding was hitched, he glanced eastwards along the valley.

A light mist was encroaching down the timbered slope on either side and visibility was already drastically reduced. So he was unable to see far enough out along the trail to catch sight of the slow-rolling string of wagons.

Not until he reached his horse, unhitched him and swung up into the saddle to heel him out across the high and barren plain did the Virginian consider the possibility that the sound of the exchange of rifle fire had carried down the valley to the Aaronites. And frightened them into turning their wagons around and heading back to find the way into a heaven on earth by another route.

But he doubted that this had happened. And could visualise the six Conestogas still crawling along the misty trail in the same direction as before. Aaron Curtain and his most fervid followers as single-minded and blindly faithful as ever. While the more practically minded would suffer a cold sweat of fear all the way to the point where he had piled the dead Paiutes and stacked their rifles.

'And you know what those crazy people will most likely do?' the Virginian rasped.

The gelding pricked his ears to the sound of his rider's voice.

'Bury the dead and toss the rifles into the brush. Hold a service, maybe.'

The gelding raised his tail and began to lay out a line of droppings.

Steele spread the boyish grin across his face and murmured: 'Is that your opinion of them or me, feller?'

CHAPTER NINE

THE RAIN held off, but Steele donned his slicker against the mist which was of the kind that was capable of soaking a man through to the skin before he was aware of it.

When dusk came, he could see no more than twenty feet and because of the sparseness of vegetation on the high plain it would have been difficult to stay on the trail but for the fact that it was clearly marked with recent sign. Many shod horses had moved in both directions along this stretch of trail and he guessed this meant he was getting close to the isolated army post of Fort St James – close enough to be within the eastern range of patrols from the fort.

'Ain't much of a place and don't reckon it'll be there very long,' the grizzled old fur trapper had told him. 'The army, anyway. And knowin' the army the way I do, there's a good chance they'll tear the place down and haul it off with 'em when they leave. Real old place it is, son. Built there first to protect people like me from the Shoshone and Paiutes who didn't take kindly to us trappers. But there never was too many hostiles that far up in the mountains. Just a band of renegades here and there. Not enough to make a fort worthwhile.

'Then some minin' men were checkin' for gold and silver up near there. Big company men, you understand. Not your hopin'-to-strike-it-lucky prospectors. After that, some big money men with government connections sent crews into the area to survey for a railroad. They came up empty, same as the minin' fellers.

'After that was all done, the blue-bellies at Fort St James didn't have nobody and nothin' to protect except themselves and their post. Reason the post is still there is that back in Washington the top brass is considerin' turnin' old St James into an army penitentiary. For them soldier boys that go bad in the Department of the West and the Department of Oregon military areas. Been tryin' to make up their minds about it for better than two years now.

'Feelin' of most of the men assigned to St James is that the place is already a prison. And they been sentenced to go there even though they ain't done nothin' wrong.

'It ain't a happy place, son. And me and fellers like me who trap in these mountains, we go there only when we gotta. And we don't spend no time there unless we gotta.'

With the night came the rain which after a few minutes turned to sleet, driven by a wind from out of the north-west. But by that time the Virginian had glimpsed a splash of yellow lamplight up ahead. And even if he had known the old furtrapper was understating the situation at Fort St James he would still have used every ounce of concentration to home in on the light that was seen for just a moment before the weather blotted it out.

The wind, although it was bitingly cold and acted to drive the icy sleet in under his hat brim and hurl it against his bristled face, was welcome. For it streamed in constantly from the north-west quarter and thus helped him to maintain a bearing on the direction of the briefly seen light.

Then sleet became snow and he seemed to be riding too far into a yielding wall of slanting whiteness: over a rapidly deepening carpet of white. Began to doubt that he had actually seen the glimmer of light through the mist earlier. To wonder if he had imagined it because it or some other sign of the fort's existence was what he wanted to see before he became totally disorientated in the storm.

But then he drew back his lips to momentarily expose his teeth in a grin – as he heard a bugler sounding the call to chow. And a few seconds later, through the snowflakes clinging to his eyelashes, saw a blurred impression of the light.

'That you and your men, Lieutenant March?' a man called.

The light gleamed some twenty feet above ground level and the words were yelled down from the same elevation.

'No, soldier!' the Virginian shouted through the funnel of a gloved hand as his path was blocked by a double gate made of split pine logs. 'A civilian! Name's Adam Steele!'

'Corporal, open the gates!'

'Yessir, captain!'

Steele swung out of the saddle and found that he sank more than ankle deep into the snow as one of the gates creaked open a couple of feet. And the corporal peered out to ask:

'You ridin' a horse or a wagon, mister?'

'Just a horse, soldier.'

'So you can squeeze in through here. The friggin' snow's driftin' high this side.'

'Grateful to you.'

The Virginian led the gelding through the narrow opening as the captain on the walkway above the gate snarled:

'We all have problems, corporal! Your detail is to keep the entrance to the fort clear! Do it instead of griping about it! After you've escorted the visitor to the post command office and attended to the stabling of his mount!'

'Yessir!' the corporal responded in the appropriate tone, but he grimaced his true feelings at Steele as he shoved the gate closed and slid a plank to fasten it. 'This way, mister.'

The Virginian trudged in his wake on a direct line across the compound, getting just a vague impression of the buildings that formed the fort within the stockade walls. For although several lamps gleamed and the walls on two sides acted to subdue the full force of the wind which slanted the snow from out of the night sky, it was still difficult to see anything clearly.

He could smell woodsmoke and cooking food and boiling coffee. And felt much colder because of this.

The corporal veered off the straight line to go around a ceremonial cannon. Then halted and turned to face Steele at the front of a long, single storey building with a pitched roof that jutted out over a raised stoop.

'If you go through that door, mister, and follow

your nose, you'll find Major Jones who's officer of the day. I'll have the stable detail take care of your horse and one of them will bring your gear to the guest barrack.'

He took the reins from Steele.

'Grateful to you.'

'Just followin' normal procedure, mister.' His youthful face showed an embittered smile. 'And I guess I oughta thank you. For gettin' me out from under the eagle eye of that mean-hearted Captain Averill. For a couple of minutes at least.'

'Corporal Zeller!' Averill's voice boomed through the sounds of the storm. 'Attend to your orders and quit the chitchat!'

The smile became a scowl. 'It's said he can read a man's mind from a mile away.'

'Or maybe he just knows his men well?' Steele suggested.

'Whichever, mister. It's a wonder he can ever get to sleep. For worryin' about which of us will work up the guts to kill the bastard.'

He led the gelding into the swirling snow to the right and Steele stepped up on to the stoop and let himself into the building: immediately relishing the stove-heated warmth of the interior.

The door gave on to a square office with a desk angled across one corner and a pot-bellied stove in another. File cabinets were aligned halfway along one wall. Maps and framed photographs were hung on all walls. There were two doors in the rear wall and one to either side. Tonight the office was dimly lit by a wedge of light that entered through the cracked-open doorway on the left. The smells of coffee and hot food wafted in from the same source.

'Whoever you are, you better be sent by the

general,' a man growled from the lamplit room. 'Interruptions ruin my digestion.'

Steele took off his slicker and hat and scattered melting snow to the floor as he crossed to the door and pushed it open wide.

'Captain Averill told me to report to you, major,' he said evenly. 'I'd just as soon be at the mess hall.'

The duty officer's room was smaller than the one Steele stepped out of. Crowded with just a desk, two chairs and a file cabinet. No maps on the walls. Just several duty rosters.

Jones was six feet tall and heavily built. He had a short neck and a fleshy, ruddy-hued face with bushy grey sideburns jutting down from under his battered campaign hat. He had slightly bulbous brown eyes and pouted lips. He probably smiled sometimes, but it was hard to visualise such an expression fitting comfortably on such a face.

He was finishing a meal of stew, soaking up the gravy with bread. A mug of steaming coffee stood on the uncluttered desk beside his near-empty plate.

'You here on official business?' the major asked as he watched Steele unbutton the sheepskin coat – and arched his eyebrows at sight of the worse-for-wear city style suit that was revealed beneath.

'No, major. Just passing through and grateful for a place to shelter from the storm.'

'You don't look like any trapper or prospector I ever saw, mister.'

'I'm not either.'

'Figured you for a government man.' He popped a final piece of gravy sodden bread into his mouth and swallowed it whole. 'Passing through from where to where? And I don't ask out of idle curiosity, mister.

We have a patrol out and overdue. A lieutenant and five men. Didn't run into them, did you?'

'No, major. Followed the trail in from the east. Didn't see any soldiers until I reached the fort.'

Jones appeared to lose interest in his visitor as he sipped at his coffee. But then a thought occurred to him. 'You say you didn't see any army men, mister? Am I to infer that you saw –'

'Some Paiutes and a group of religious people who call themselves Aaronites. If the storm lets up, the Aaronites could reach here during the night.'

'Paiutes?'

'Ten of them, major.'

'White Fox and his bunch of troublemakers. They give you any trouble, mister?'

'Only of my own making.'

The officer directed a glower of impatience at Steele. 'This is an army post, mister. It's our duty to offer comforts to civilians in need. But once inside the gates of Fort St James civilians are required to do things the army way. So if you have a report to make on any incident concerning security within the jurisdiction of this post, make it. Don't hand me riddles, mister.'

The Virginian draped his coat and slicker across the top of the file cabinet and placed his Stetson on top. Then dropped into the chair at the front of the desk.

'Yes, mister, you have my permission to sit down,' Jones growled sarcastically. 'If it'll help you to give a clear and concise account of your run-in with the hostiles.'

Steele pursed his lips and allowed a short sigh to rasp out. Then said evenly: 'I'm cold, I'm tired and I'm hungry, major. So you can be sure this is going to be concise. And I'll do my best to make it clear so we don't have to waste time with questions after I'm through.'

Jones bristled with anger. 'May I remind you that I am a major in the army of the United States and insist that while you are on a military establishment you will give me the respect that my rank commands!'

Steele made no direct response to this, but launched straight into an account of what had happened since he heard the Paiutes attacking the wagon train a day and a half ago. Not until he was through and rose from the chair did he refer to the major's attempt to bawl him out.

'I've served army time myself, Major Jones. So I don't need any lessons in military etiquette. I have respect for your uniform and badges of rank. Just happen to think that the man wearing them is a lousy host. Which could be why I'm acting like a bad guest.'

The officer's anger did not rise again. Instead, he continued to eye the Virginian with astonishment. And although he waited for Steele to complete the afterword to his report, he seemed to hear only the sound of the Virginian's voice: to be oblivious to the sense of what was being said to him as he struggled to come to terms with something he had already heard.

'You wiped out White Fox and the whole of his band singlehanded, mister?'

'Like I told you, not all at one time, major,' the Virginian answered as he rose from the chair. 'And it wasn't just killing Paiutes that gave me an appetite.'

'General Dubois should know of this.'

'If you want me to do it, do you think the general would mind if I was eating at the same time?'

'Of course, of course,' Major Jones murmured absently. Then he reached behind him and tugged on a length of rope that hung down the wall at the back of his chair. This caused a low toned bell to clang twice on the roof of the building. 'I'd be obliged if you would answer one further question for me?'

Steele was on the threshold of the room, his hat back on his head and the slicker draping his shoulders, topcoat under an arm.

'Sure, major.'

The door from the compound opened to admit an enlisted man and a blast of snowy night air.

'Wait, soldier!' Jones barked. Then asked of the Virginian: 'The Paiutes? Did they have scalps on their belts? Or were they wearing any items of army issue clothing?'

'No, major.'

'Weapons?'

'Winchesters and some old side arms.'

Jones squeezed his eyes tight closed and sighed. Growled to himself: 'So the bastards deserted, I'll bet.' Then he shook off morose anger to bark: 'Soldier!'

'Yessir!'

'Show Mr Steele to the guest barrack. Then have one of the cooks bring him a meal. After that, return to this office and wait. Anyone needs me, I'll be with General Dubois. But there better be damn good reason to need me.'

'Yessir! If you'll come this way, Mr Steele.'

The Virginian turned on the threshold.

Jones said: 'If a runner does not come for you within fifteen minutes, feel free to bed down, mister. The general won't require to see you.'

He was soured by bitter anger again: preoccupied with the ramifications of desertion. Was close behind Steele and the enlisted man as they went out of the building. Turned left as the soldier indicated the civilian visitor to the post should head right along the stoop.

'How long overdue are Lieutenant March and his patrol, feller?'

'Left the post at eight this mornin' and oughta have been back at noon, sir.'

'Desertion not common at St James?'

'The men talk about it a lot, sir. But ain't no one ever tried it in my tour of duty here. This way, sir.'

He led the way down off the stoop and then angled across a gap between the side of the administration building and the front of what smelled like the stables. The snow was more than a foot deep now. Deeper at the front of a small shack where the eddying wind had drifted it.

Inside, the soldier lit a ceiling-hung kerosene lamp and carried the still flaring match to a stove. Where he squatted to start a ready laid fire.

'Take your pick, sir. Ain't no other civilians stayin' right now. Chow'll be here pretty soon.'

'Grateful to you.'

'Just followin' orders.'

He went out and closed the door behind him: another young soldier with precisely the same attitude as Corporal Zeller. Resentfully polite as he followed his orders: maybe envious of the visitor's civilian status.

The guest barrack was longer than it was wide. There were five beds along the rear wall and two to each side of the door, partitioned off from floor to ceiling but open to the aisle down the centre of the room. The stove was midway along the aisle. There was a table at each end. One ringed by four chairs and the other bearing two basins and pitchers.

Steele stepped into the cubicle where his saddle and bedroll lay on the floor in a pool of water which had drained off them. And spent a little time hanging everything that was wet on hooks aligned along the partition on one side of the bed.

He was wiping excess moisture off the Colt Hartford and beginning to experience the warmth of the stove when a fist thudded on the door, which swung open a moment later, and the heat was dissipated as a fat corporal with a black beard entered: bearing a tray with a cover draped over it.

'Welcome to the St James Ritz,' the man growled as he back-heeled the door closed. 'With room service at no extra charge.'

He went down the aisle to lower the tray to the chair ringed table.

'I'm just following orders, feller,' Steele told him. 'And so are you, so I won't thank you.'

The corporal had dead-looking dark eyes and warts on his cheeks where his beard did not grow. The scowl seemed to be a permanent fixture on his ugly face.

'And I figure no one on this post has reason to thank you, mister. If you really did knock off old White Fox and his bunch.'

Steele sat down on the chair with the tray in front of him. Lifted the cover and saw what Major Jones' meal had looked like before the officer ate it. It smelled good.

'What would be the point of me lying, feller?' He started to eat the beef stew that tasted as good as he expected.

'None, I figure,' the corporal allowed with a shrug. 'Just that I ain't never seen no dude Indian fighter before.'

'You're not seeing one now. It was just something personal between the Paiutes and me. Way it happened, they didn't know it.'

The fat soldier shrugged again. 'It don't matter. Young Mayer didn't hear enough of what was said between you and the major to find out how it happened. And me and most other men on the post don't care too much, anyway. But you should know you didn't do us any favour when you sent them redskins to the happy huntin' ground.'

'Never occurred to me that I did.'

The corporal sat his broad rump on the end of a bed, took a half smoked cigar from inside his greatcoat and lit it. 'This friggin' place shouldn't be here. Ain't no need of it but the brass-hats back east keep tryin' to figure out reasons to have men here.'

'Feller who told me there was a post here said there was a plan to make it an army prison.'

'That's the last we heard, mister. But it ain't come to be yet. And that gets up the nose of the general we got commandin' us. Who don't like being at St James no more than everyone else here. But because he's a general, he can do somethin' about it.

'So he comes up with a reason to be here. Old White Fox and the rest of them asshole redskins who for most of the time never do nothin' except hunt in the hills. But three times, far as we know, they hit white folks. One was a trapper they just held up to steal his liquor and grub. Then a couple of bug-eyed tourists. Man and wife who come into the mountains to paint pictures, would you believe? Stole their supplies and took the wife. Had their way with her for a week or so and turned her loose. Didn't do nothin' to the husband except knock him around a little. Them Winchesters they had, they got them off a gunrunner. Killed him, and that wasn't nothin' more than he deserved.'

Steele had finished the stew and was sipping the

strong coffee. 'Never did claim to the major that I'd killed the toughest bunch of Indians I've ever come across, feller.'

The scowl became more firmly set on the bearded face. 'That ain't how the general will see it, mister. Them Paiutes was guilty of stealin' from whites, beatin' up a white man, rapin' a white woman and murder. And, worse of all, we never was able to get close enough to them to take a shot at them. You know why, mister?'

The corporal rose and came to take the tray away from Steele – and stubbed out his cigar on the greasy plate.

'I can guess, feller.'

'So guess,' came the challenge.

'Because you didn't want to.'

The fat and ugly soldier was surprised. Steele finished the coffee and reached out to set the empty mug on the tray.

'While White Fox was out riding free in the mountains he kept the general busy. Kept him from brooding about how a man of his rank got to be assigned to a post that doesn't merit any officer above major being in command.'

'That's friggin' right, mister,' was the sour voiced response. 'The general's been in this man's army since he was old enough to be a drummer boy. Been in a lot of shit campaigns but never made a name for himself. Blames everyone but himself for that and out here there ain't nobody else to blame except the officers and men under him.'

Steele left the table to return to his chosen cubicle. Asked: 'Was that the hearty meal for a condemned man before the general hangs me for killing his reason for living?'

'You ain't got nothin' to worry about, mister. Soon as the storm lets up, you'll be able to ride outta here. But we have to stay. And Dubois will get back to bein' like he was before White Fox and his bunch moved into the area. It'll be all drills and inspections. Policing the post and survival treks in the mountains. Weapons practise and lectures on every friggin' thing. With horseshit on your boot when you come outta the stable enough to get you on friggin' report.

'We'll be like we used to be. The fittest, neatest, brainiest friggin' company in the whole friggin' army. And for what? Frig all is what!'

Steele had sat down on the bed to complete cleaning the Colt Hartford. And gave only partial attention to the embittered opinion of the corporal as he heard a din of shouting out on the fort compound.

The soldier with the tray paused as he was about to open the door and moderated his tone. 'No hard feelin's, mister. You had your reasons for killin' them redskins and that's your business. I just run off at the mouth so you won't be disappointed if no one shows you any appreciation for what you done.'

The Virginian leaned the rifle into the angle of the wall and a partition of the cubicle.

'No way you could have known what a crazy sonofabitch Dubois is.'

'Sure, feller. But I reckon that now I've got a bad general impression.'

CHAPTER TEN

THE WIND that blew into the guest barrack while the corporal had the door open was less forceful than earlier. And the snowfall was more subdued. Not so many voices were yelling, and against the diminished sounds of the storm Steele could hear hooves thudding in the snow, the creak of harness and the jingle of spurs.

But the Virginian did not go to one of the misted-up windows to see what was happening out on the compound. Instead, he moved away from the bed simply to turn out the lamp. Then undressed to his pants, socks and shirt in the dim light of the stove's glow and slid under the bedcovers.

From outside came an order to open the gates of the fort. Then a command for riders to move forward. Horses snorted and pounded at the deep snow – maybe up to a dozen of them. The gates creaked closed and no further sounds intruded into the guest barrack. Where Adam Steele lay in the comfort of the bed, his body warmth gradually negating the initial damp feel of the blankets. He made no conscious effort to keep his mind free of unwelcome thoughts. But experienced no curiosity about the purpose of the late night mission from Fort St James. Nor chagrin that the success of his lone assault on the Paiutes had met with virtually universal dismay.

He simply had a sense of well-being because of the contrast in his situation to what it had been little more than an hour ago, when there had been a real danger of freezing to death out on the high plain. And now he was well fed, had a roof over his head, a stove to warm him and a clean bed to sleep in.

So he slept.

Woke to the sound of the bugler's reveille which rang out clearly within the confines of the stockade: not needing to compete with the howl of the north-west wind.

Steele had total and instant recall the moment he snapped open his eyes. And knew somebody had entered the guest barrack of Fort St James during the night. For the degree of heat in the room owed nothing to the watery, early morning sunlight that slanted through the south-facing window. So more fuel had been put into the stove.

Then, when he was out of bed, he saw that a pot of water had been placed on top of the stove. He used this to wash up and shave in one of the basins at the end of the room. Then dressed in everything except his hat and gloves. Was about to don these when the door swung open and a man brought in his breakfast tray. But it was not the fat and bearded corporal this morning. Instead a tall, emaciatedly thin, clean shaven man. His uniform bearing the insignia of a general.

'Good day to you, Mr Steele. I am Gerald Dubois. I trust you slept well?'

The Virginian had not come face to face with a general since the War Between the States. And it surprised him that he had to consciously subdue an impulse to come to rigid attention. An instinct to which he had never been prone when he came across the officers of lesser rank who commanded other isolated military posts where he had briefly stayed.

'It was fine, sir. I'm grateful for your hospitality.'

The general, who was close to sixty and had a burnished, deeply-lined face which would have been handsome with more flesh, took the tray to the table at the far end of the aisle.

'We do the best we are able for the infrequent visitors we have, Mr Steele.' He rested the tray and sat down in a chair on the opposite side of the table. And smiled a smile that did not fit with his reputation as a martinet. 'Although our facilities do not normally extend to having breakfast served by the general commanding.'

He removed the tray cover to reveal a plate of bacon, beans and grits and two mugs of coffee. He claimed one of the mugs for himself as the Virginian sat down.

'Exceptional circumstances, sir?'

The smile went from his thin features. 'You are an exceptional man, Mr Steele. I was interested to meet you. Please go on and eat.'

The Virginian did so, noting that Dubois looked neat and bright despite the early hour.

'White Fox and his band have been a thorn in our flesh here for a very long time.'

'So I heard, sir.'

A dark scowl spread across the angular features of the officer. 'From good-for-nothing incompetents who were themselves unable to rid this area of the savages.'

'Sometimes one man is better suited to a task than an entire army, general.'

Dubois vented a throaty sound of disgust. And showed his true colours when he snarled 'It is not for you to make excuses for the men of this post, Steele!'

'Wasn't doing that,' the Virginian answered evenly. 'Just stating a fact that I believe in. Do you believe what I told Major Jones last night?'

The thin general was still bristling. 'You have reason to think I doubt your word?'

'I heard a patrol leave the post last night. It occurred to me this morning the men may have been despatched to check that –'

'You told the duty officer of a wagon train of civilians within the jurisdiction of Fort St James, Mr Steele. Women and children along. In view of the storm, I ordered a patrol out to see if those people required assistance.'

'A prime tenet of the Aaronites is that God will provide all the help they need.'

Dubois snorted again. 'The Almighty created those Paiute savages, Mr Steele. Who would have certainly destroyed these crazy Aaronites but for your intervention. He also made it snow last night. But I did not come here to discuss theological beliefs in a harshly realistic world. I have a request to make of you.'

'Whatever I can, general.'

The officer appeared abruptly embarrassed. He cleared his throat. 'I apologise for my rudeness a few moments ago. Your theory that in certain circumstances a numerically superior force is not necessarily the most expedient tactic to adopt against the enemy has some credence . . . .' He cleared his throat again. Asked: 'You appear to be of an age that made you suitable for war service, is that true?'

'I was a cavalry lieutenant, general.'

'Ah, excellent. You had battle experience, I trust?'

'My fair share.'

'That will make it more interesting. Give greater authority to what you have to say. You will be able to relate your civilian Indian-fighting episodes to the military theatre of operations.'

'I will, general? When?'

Recalling something the fat corporal had told him in predicting the future at Fort St James, Steele could guess at what was in the mind of Dubois.

'Ah, in my enthusiasm, I neglected to put my request. What I'd like is for you to address the men. Take them step by step through your strategy in overcoming the savages.'

The Virginian rattled his fork down on the empty plate and drank some coffee, aware of the brightly eager eyes of the other man gazing fixedly at him.

'You have any kind of charity box here, general? For widows and orphans maybe?'

Dubois' eyes were abruptly puzzled as he shook his head. 'I don't understand, Mr Steele.'

'I've been well taken care of here at the post. And I always prefer to pay for what I've had. Prepared to give a fair price to any cause you happen to support. Not prepared to stand up in front of a company of army men and shoot off my mouth about how I killed a bunch of Indians who meant me no harm.'

It was no longer embarrassment that trapped words in the throat of Dubois. Instead, the constricting effect of high anger. Which was not negated until after he had slammed his mug down on the table, spilling coffee, and powered to his feet.

'Mister, you're out of line!' he snarled. 'If you were under my command I'd –'

'But I'm not, general,' Steele put in evenly. 'And unless you have any other plans in which I can agree to take part, I'll –'

'You will leave Fort St James with the utmost speed!' General Dubois snapped. 'The men here have sufficient distractions among themselves to strain the rules of discipline. They do not need you as an example of crass insubordination.'

He strode along the aisle and wrenched open the door. Paused to bark: 'You are a sad disappointment to me, Mr Steele.'

Then he hurried angrily out of the guest barrack without looking back through the doorway he left open behind him.

Steele followed a few seconds later. The Colt Hartford back in the boot and his gear hefted under one arm, Stetson tipped forward to shade his eyes from the early morning sun that shone without heat from out of a cloudless sky.

Beyond where it had drifted at the front of the barrack the snow was just a little more than a foot deep. Except out on the centre of the compound, where a dozen soldiers dressed in fatigues were working with brushes and shovels to clear it.

'The general don't look happy,' a man said as Steele made to turn into the stable.

It was the young Corporal Zeller, who came out of the stable carrying a shovel.

'It seems I'm a disappointment to him,' the Virginian answered.

Zeller started to shovel snow from the stable entrance. 'Life's one big disappointment to the general, mister,' he growled with a scowling glance across the front of the administration building, where Dubois stood on the stoop surveying the snow clearing activity. 'What'd he want you to do, join this man's army?'

On all sides of the compound, men clad in fatigues were emerging from the various buildings with shovels and brushes to join in the snow clearance operation. And went to work with obvious reluctance for the chore, which did not improve the general's glinting eyed bad humour.

'He may be crazy, feller, but not that crazy.'

Steele entered the stable, found the gelding and saddled him. Noting that, like the section of the administration building he saw and the guest barrack, the stable was neat and cleanly kept. Which was a measure of the commanding officer's success in running this isolated outpost with disgruntled men serving an unpopular tour of duty at the out-moded and dilapidated Fort St James.

'Captain Averill's patrol is returnin' to the post, sir!' a man roared.

'Well, open the gates for them, sergeant!' Dubois bellowed back.

'Open the gates below!'

'Nobody told you men to stop work!' The general sounded as intractable as ever.

'Hard nosed sonofabitch,' Zeller growled as Steele led his well fed and rested gelding out of the stable. And it was not the only low-voiced insult directed at the tall, thin figure of Dubois striding across the compound from the administration building to the gate. For against the creaking of the big gates being opened, the body of vocal resentment sounded as a sibilant hiss that the general could not fail to hear.

But the ramrod erect officer ignored it and Steele's estimation of the man rose.

'General, sir, they're haulin' in a wagon!' the non-com on the walkway above the fort entrance announced.

Standing at ease immediately in the gap of the open gateway, Dubois retorted: 'The army of the United States does not entrust the command of a fort to a blind man, sergeant!'

'Crusty as month old bread, ain't he, Mr Steele,' Zeller muttered.

'But I reckon he knows how to cut it around here, feller,' the Virginian answered as he led the gelding away from the stable.

During the storm, Corporal Zeller had kept the area immediately behind the gates clear of the snow and the middle-aged, medium built and round faced Captain Averill was the first to ride on to the patch of frozen ground as Dubois moved to the side.

The lower rank officer threw up a salute to the general, but his frowning eyes shifted their attention away from Dubois as soon as the acknowledgement was given. And remained fixed upon the approaching Virginian as he snapped:

'One wagon stripped of supplies, sir! Five dead civilians aboard! Looks like the work of White Fox and his band, sir!'

Two enlisted men rode through the gateway, followed by a Conestoga hauled by a team that was close to exhaustion. A sergeant was in charge of the wagon, his mount hitched to the tailgate. Two enlisted men brought up the rear and the gates were creaked closed behind them.

The snow clearing details risked being on the receiving end of the general's anger as they halted their chore to switch their expectant attention between the wagon and the Virginian: who had stopped and was gazing impassively at the bullet pitted Conestoga, unable to recognise it in terms of which Aaronite family it had belonged to. But knowing that no family had comprised five people.

Now General Dubois turned just his head to gaze at Steele, but there was no censure in his eyes.

'You made no mention of the fact that the civilians had casualties, mister,' he said flatly.

'They didn't, general. Not as a result of White Fox and his braves hitting them.'

'Then we have to assume another band of hostiles has moved into the area. That, or this wagon is not one of those from the train you spoke of.'

'Or Steele is a lying braggart, sir!' Averill added sneeringly.

'What is to be believed, mister?' Dubois asked, his tone hardening.

The Virginian led his horse closer to the wagon, angling toward the rear. 'In this case, general,' he answered evenly, 'I'm not prepared to believe in the coincidence of another band of Indians and another wagon.'

The two enlisted men who had been riding drag sidled their mounts out of his path. And Steele put one foot in the stirrup and gripped the saddle horn but did not swing astride the gelding. Simply raised himself high enough to see over the top of the Conestoga's tailgate. The corpses were draped with army issue blankets but one of these had fallen aside to reveal the head and shoulders of an acne faced young boy who would never get to hear about Abraham Lincoln and how he came to give a rifle to Adam Steele's father.

'Well, mister?' Dubois demanded insistently as Steele lowered himself to the ground.

'And I don't believe there's a ghost of a chance White Fox hit this wagon.'

CHAPTER ELEVEN

THE CONESTOGA was the one which had been allocated to Bradley and Grace Horan back in the small Pennsylvania town from which the chosen group of Aaronites had set out westwards to find a place free from persecution.

The middle-aged Horans now lay in the post mortuary. Along with Tommy and Joel Rycott who in life had ridden with their parents. And Irene Boucher, the spinster who had shared a wagon with her brother-in-law and sister, Paul and Gertrude Mayne.

All of them had been shot, some more than once, and their corpses were frozen stiff: the blood on their clothing turned to ice.

Steele impassively identified each body before it was carried into the mortuary. Where it would not remain for long – a grave digging detail was already at work just outside the south wall of the stockade. While the Virginian sat at the clerk's desk in the otherwise empty anteroom of the administration building. Drinking coffee and listening to the conference which Dubois was holding in the command post office.

Captain Averill had given his report on the discovery of the wagon and now Dubois was briefing the two lower rank officers on his plan to deal with the situation – concentrating on the known facts and checking Averill's attempts at speculation.

The Virginian's name was not mentioned as he sat in the stove heat of the room and had to make a conscious effort not to indulge in conjecture himself. Beyond gaining an impression from what he heard that the general was relishing the circumstances, the major was content to go along with everything Dubois said and the captain was sullenly convinced that Steele was a liar with an ulterior motive.

Then the expressions on the faces of the three officers as they came out into the anteroom were a perfect match for the moods which the Virginian had detected in their voices.

Jones and Averill went out on to the compound; the major to attend to the burial of the dead and the captain to order a search party to prepare for leaving the fort.

The painfully thin general with the gleam in his eyes asked: 'You heard what was said in there, Mr Steele?'

'Yes, general.' He rose from the desk.

'Like you to know I have my own ideas about what happened over to the east during last night's storm. And they are based upon you telling the truth.'

'I'm not going to kiss your ass for that, general.'

Dubois was moved to anger, but he controlled it. To the extent that his tone was severe, but not harsh.

'My own ideas, but I'm not going to prejudge the issue. Offering you a choice, mister. You may either remain here on the post, unconfined within the walls of the fort on your promise not to try to leave. Or you may ride with the search party I intend to lead.'

'If I stay in one place too long, general, I get itchy feet.'

'Or if you happen to be sitting down, it's somewhere else that needs scratching, uh?'

Steele drew back his lips to show a cold smile which failed to get a like response from Dubois.

'Never been an ass-kisser myself, mister. Which is maybe why the army has put me out to grass at Fort St James.' He shook his head, mildly angry at himself. 'But that is neither here nor there. Don't expect any man from a junior general down to the rawest recruit to toady to me, mister. But having made your choice, you'll obey army regulations out there in the field. Or I'll have you sent back to the post under close escort. Any questions?'

He went toward the still open doorway.

'Just ones that can only be answered outside of the post, general.'

Dubois paused. 'You surprise me, mister. Way you've been acting so cool, calm and collected, I didn't think you gave a damn about those people being murdered. Yet you're real curious about what happened, aren't you?'

'It's no act, general,' the Virginian answered evenly. 'Those folks in the mortuary knew the risks they were running. Just that I prefer to have a front row seat rather than stay behind the scenes. Since you gave me the choice.'

'And as an added incentive, you will be able to watch Captain Averill eat crow if we track down the new villains of the piece, uh?'

'The opinions of my critics have never bothered me, general. And as far as this latest play is concerned, I have good reason to know the Paiutes took no part in it.'

Dubois made to leave the building, but pulled up short: a thoughtful frown on his face. Which transformed into a frosty smile as he warned: 'To continue the theatrical analogy, Mr Steele, I caution you to keep in mind that you will have a civilian role in what is now a military operation.'

The Virginian expressed the boyish smile that acted to make him look younger. Did not get the older man to unbend beyond the point of the half smile when he murmured: 'Let's call a halt at this stage.'

CHAPTER TWELVE

THE ROUND trip which Averill's night patrol had made to locate and bring back the corpse-laden Conestoga meant there was an easy to follow route to the scene of the killings. Hooves and wheelrims having churned up a twenty foot wide strip across the carpet of frost crisped whiteness that was spread out, undisturbed, for as far as the eye could see to either side.

Twenty-one men followed the sign, riding horses at walking pace. General Dubois and Captain Averill at the head with eighteen enlisted men and non-coms in a column of three behind. Adam Steele brought up the rear, having selected this position himself when he was not invited to take any other as the riders left the fort.

The only other soldier in the column he knew by name was Corporal Zeller who rode in the centre of the first rank behind the officers: carrying the company pennant.

The morning sun was beginning to make its warmth felt now, and after riding a mile from the post the layer of frost was melted and the disturbed snow no longer crunched under the hooves of the mounts.

The general proved to be as much a stickler for army regulations outside of Fort St James as in. Thus, every soldier was immaculately turned out and Dubois cast frequent glances over his shoulder to check that the column remained in tight formation. And if there were any exchanges between the men they were made in low tones and curtailed immediately when the general's eyes raked along the column.

So, while the fort's commanding officer was prepared to condone the age old prerogative of a soldier to gripe about routine chores, he did not allow it on a mission.

As a lowly lieutenant during the War Between the States, the Virginian had tried to apply the same tactic to the various cavalry troops he commanded. Not always with as much success as Dubois – but then this man had an age and rank advantage to support his authority. No soldier argued with an embittered elderly general nearing the end of a career that had not matched his expectations.

Steele, with only the alternative of conjecture about the fate of the Aaronites to occupy his mind, pondered a great deal about General Gerald Dubois as he rode behind the column of blue-clad soldiers moving slowly across the snow covered high plain. And concluded he could root for the old man making a success of this mission. And this not just because he had himself been an officer which aligned him against the men. Instead, because until fairly recently, he could have identified with Dubois: while he was striving to achieve something out of a life that had become nothing. Destined never to get that for which he aimed because of his stubborn refusal to make compromises.

Not prepared to bend to the whims of civilian society just as Dubois would rather do without the rewards of military conformity if they entailed abandoning his principles.

And was not Aaron Curtain cut from a similar pattern?

Steele refused to follow this train of thought. And for the remainder of the ride to the scene of the killings kept his mind as blank as his expression.

Some five miles from Fort St James, the sign left by the night patrol angled off the more or less straight line of the trail and the column veered due north. Came to a halt at a signal from Averill at the base of a rock outcrop some thirty feet high by forty long.

Only the general and the captain dismounted as Steele swung the gelding out from behind the column and rode to the fringe of a wide area of churned up snow. The sun was melting the snow now, but at two points a few feet apart there were still traces of blood to be seen as conclusive evidence that this had been a scene of violence.

'. . . was parked right here under the outcrop, sir,' Averill was saying as Steele swung from the saddle and moved within earshot. 'Team still in the traces. Like they had made it into the shelter of the rock when the storm was at its height and were waiting for it to ease before unhitching the horses. Or were hit by the Ind. . . . the attackers before they could do it.'

Averill was eyeing Steele balefully, but he sensed the general's reproachful glance and corrected himself before he completed the reference to the Paiutes.

'Wasn't snowing when you got here, is that right, captain?'

'Yessir. If it had not stopped, I guess we would have ridden right by without spotting the wagon against the outcrop. But the attackers hit during the storm.' He pointed to the bloodstains. 'That's where we found the two children, sir. Partially covered by snow. But in a way that indicated they were shot and simply left where they fell. Not buried by anybody. The man and two women were inside the wagon.'

'Not shot, captain,' Dubois said bleakly. 'Executed. Taken from the wagon, probably after the adults were dead, told to stand there. Then shot in the back of the head with a handgun.'

'Yes, sir,' Averill agreed, and swallowed hard as some of the men muttered oaths directed at the unknown killers of the two young boys. Then the captain growled: 'A *savage* act to commit, sir.'

Steele ignored the unsubtle reference to the Paiutes as he raked his gaze over the scene of the slaughter: trying to get a picture of what had happened from the sign. Which was not easy, because falling snow had masked the impressions made before, during and immediately after the attack. And the clear-to-see sign had all been left by the activities of the night patrol when they located the Conestoga.

'This telling you anything, mister?' Dubois asked after allowing the Virginian about a minute to survey the area.

'That the wagon was facing the wrong way, general,' Steele answered pensively, and began to kick at the snow. 'Back east.'

'I could have told you that,' Averill growled.

'Don't recall you mentioning it in your report, captain,' Dubois said flatly.

Averill had to suppress his anger at Steele, fearful the general might consider it was directed at him. 'It doesn't appear to be significant, sir. Perhaps the outcrop was seen after the wagon had passed on the trail and the driver made a wide swing to gain its shelter. Or there could have been a running fight that ended here. The attackers attempted to hold up the wagon on the trail and the driver turned and attempted to outrun –'

'What significance do you feel it has, mister?' Dubois cut in.

This as Steele's boot hit something under the snow close to the base of the outcrop. Squatted down and delved with a gloved hand – to draw out a Winchester.

There was no way to tell if it was one of the rifles he had stacked on the trail close to the heap of dead Paiutes at the head of the valley to the east.

'I reckon you should have the men check the area to the north of this outcrop, general,' the Virginian answered as he began to pump the action of the repeater. Grunted as the magazine was emptied by just six live bullets spinning out to lie in the snow.

'I would have to know why you ask,' Dubois said.

Steele dropped the Winchester among the ejected shells in the sun-softened snow. 'The driver of the wagon – Brad Horan – was one of the Aaronites in favour of having me ride shotgun on the train. So was the old lady, Irene Boucher. And Clinton Rycott who was the father of the two boys. Don't know how Mrs Horan felt about it, but I reckon she was the kind of wife who went along with her husband's way of thinking.

'What I reckon happened was that the wagons swung off the trail somewhere west of the head of the valley. Then the snow came and enough of the Aaronites were against pressing on for a meeting to be called. They call it a convocation. Brad Horan was set on turning back. The Boucher woman asked to go along. And Rycott asked the Horans if they would take his boys. They got this far and no further.'

'And we should scour the ground to the north because the outcrop is north of the trail?' Dubois guessed.

'It's a starting point, general.'

'Sir?' Averill snapped.

'What is it, captain?'

'Assuming the civilian is correct in his supposition, that is no reason to also suppose the killers went north from here.'

There were some sounds of grudging approval from the men: silenced by a flinty glare from Dubois. Who then said to Averill with scorn:

'Captain, you have the priorities wrong. It is the civilians aboard the other five wagons who are our main concern. Who are still in grave danger even if the killers are long gone. You have patrolled these mountains often enough to be aware that they are capable of killing without the help of evil men.' He swung his head, shifting his gaze from the chagrined face of Averill to instruct: 'Sergeant, dismount the troop and search the area to either end and at the north of the outcrop.'

'Yessir!'

The greatcoated men got from their saddles on the order of the general and split into two groups of nine to start scouring the unhelpful carpet of slowly melting snow.

Averill lit a cheroot after gesturing for permission and receiving a nod from Dubois. Then the captain moved the discarded rifle with a toe of his boot. Asked:

'You can't say if this was one of the hostile's rifles, mister?'

'No, captain. If it was, it must have been brought here by somebody aboard the wagon. Maybe it was half empty. Or maybe one of the adults overcame religious convictions and fired up to six shots at the attackers.'

Dubois sighed and massaged his brow with a finger and thumb. He no longer looked bright and fresh: his age and lack of flesh to help insulate him against the cold already taking its toll.

'If I felt able to spare you, captain,' the general said wearily, 'I'd be happy to have you ride to where Steele claims he left the bodies of the Indians. Even though I am increasingly convinced that material proof of his account is unnecessary.'

'You ready to put into words now what you're also convinced of, general?' the Virginian asked evenly.

Dubois grimaced.

Averill looked set to snarl an angry retort.

From the western end of the outcrop, a man shouted: 'Sergeant, sergeant! Come over here! Holy Mother of God!'

Not only the sergeant ran toward the shouting man. All nine members of the search party in the area of the discovery were gathered into a group as Steele, Dubois and Averill came close enough to see what had been found.

The frozen corpse of a uniformed soldier with corporal's chevrons on his sleeve. Just half his torso and head in view after the man who found him had scraped away some of the drifted snow that had buried him at the base of the rock.

'Bill Grimes,' an enlisted man said huskily.

Zeller squatted to scrape away some more snow: to reveal where a bullet had penetrated the right side of his fellow corporal's chest. To enter the lung, from the frozen blood that showed in the gaped open mouth of the dead face.

'It appears there is no necessity for me to do as you asked, mister,' Dubois said bitterly. Then, to Averill: 'I'm sorry, captain.'

The lower rank officer was ashen-faced as he stared down at the corpse. And seemed unaware the cheroot had dropped from his lips to sizzle out in the snow. But he could not be oblivious to the bile which rose to his throat: and managed to swing around and gain some kind of privacy at the base of the rock before the threat of nausea became reality and he vomited his last meal.

'Mount the men, sergeant,' Dubois said quietly. 'We'll take a look around up at Three Peaks Pass.'

'What about Corporal Grimes, sir?'

'Cover him with snow again and mark the spot. We'll attend to what is necessary later.'

The orders were complied with.

'Join us when you are ready, captain,' Dubois invited.

'If you'll just give me a moment, sir.'

His stomach was empty and he was using handfuls of snow to wash his face.

'It wasn't just the fact of facing up to desertion that forced him to convince himself I was lying, general?' Steele said as he and Dubois moved away from Averill.

'Nor the sight of a dead man that made him sick to his stomach, Mr Steele. One of the other five men in Lieutenant March's patrol was Trooper Miles Averill. The captain's younger brother.'

The captain caught up with them as the men were swinging astride their mounts.

'My apologies, sir,' he said. 'And to you, also, mister. I feel utterly disgusted with myself.'

'Forget it, captain,' Steele told him.

'And keep in mind that your brother was the rawest recruit we had at the fort,' Dubois added. 'Under the command of a sour tempered officer. And riding the patrol with four of the most long-serving men at St James. Do not attempt to pre-judge the issue until we know all the facts.'

'Yessir.'

Dubois got stiffly into his saddle. 'And meantime, captain, we must all concentrate our attention on locating the civilians. Let's move out.'

Averill gave the hand signal and the column started off, Steele riding alongside the two officers at its head now. Along the south facing side of the outcrop and then snaking around the western end to strike out due north towards a distant range of ridges.

'Is there something special about Three Peaks Pass, general?' Steele asked of the elderly man who rode on his right, flanked on the other side by the captain.

'It is the only way to get beyond that high ground you can see, mister. And this late in the year it is often not a way at all.'

'And on the other side of the mountains?'

'Three Peaks Pass is the white man's name. The Nez Perce Indians who used to be pretty thick on the ground hereabouts had their own name for it. Came from the fact that to the north of that range is a deep, wide valley of fertile land that gets snowed in but where there is very little precipitation. Plenty of melt-water rivers, though.

'Closest the linguistic scholars can get to a translation of the Nez Perce name is Gate Through the Mountains of Purgatory into the Land of Just Rewards.'

He turned his emaciated face toward Steele, a quizzical expression in his no longer bright eyes. Said: 'Perhaps this man they call the padre really does have a spiritual guide. And those unfortunates buried under the south wall of St James were punished because of their lack of faith at such a late hour.'

'It's a thought, general.'

'At which realists such as we are inclined to scoff, uh?'

Steele eyed the ominous line of snow-draped rock ridges impassively. 'Never scoff at a man's religious beliefs, general.'

'While not believing yourself that mortal man is blessed with an eternal soul?'

'Reckon that some mortal men not a million miles from here, general, are assholes.'

CHAPTER THIRTEEN

THE SKY remained clear blue and during what remained of the morning the bright sun continued its slow melt of the snow. But while the men and horses rested for thirty minutes a little after midday the temperature dropped. And although the sun stayed bright for most of its slide down the south-western sky, the snow became crunchy under the hooves of the horses and the vapour of breath expelled by men and mounts was more apparent in the otherwise crystal clear air.

The mountains to which the column was riding had no foothills. The high plain came to an abrupt end and the rock faces reared up sheer to either side of what appeared to be the fifty feet wide entrance to a canyon, the flanking cliffs rising more than a hundred feet to the rims.

But it was just a trick of the fading light at sundown that made the formation look like a canyon. In fact, the cliff to the left was at the base of one mountain, and that to the right, a curving slab of rock jutting from another: to form a circular indentation at the edge of the range.

Because of the reflecting effect of the snow, the light of the near full moon was almost as good as that of the sun and the men who rode into the encirclement of towering rock were able to examine their surroundings in detail.

The ground was level over most of the area, but rose sharply diagonally across from the southern entrance: at the start of a natural trail that started to head north but curved west and went from sight.

Three Conestoga wagons were parked on the flat ground at the foot of the trail, minus their teams.

'Check them out, sergeant,' Averill ordered, and his voice echoed eerily within the rock walls.

The senior non-com signalled for Corporal Zeller and two enlisted men to go with him. Each of them drew the Springfield rifle from his boot and unfastened the flap on his holster after sliding from the saddle.

The army men who remained mounted divided their tense attention between the wagons and the high ground on almost every side. Each experiencing a sensation of claustrophobia and a fear they were better able to understand – of being shot at by a hidden enemy. So many hands reached forward to gain some kind of comfort from touching the ice cold stocks of booted rifles.

'Conestogas were built for the flat terrain of the east,' General Dubois said evenly and, despite the echo effect, his matter-of-fact tone acted to reduce the tension within some of the men. 'Too damn heavy for mountain country.'

'Nobody told us that, mister!' a man announced weakly.

Which caused the men closing with the wagons to come to an abrupt halt and swing their rifles. Toward the centre wagon in the line of three which became the focal point of every pair of eyes.

'Hold your fire!' Steele snapped. Then: 'That you, Mr Mayne?'

'Steele? Adam Steele?' Paul Mayne came back. And there was a degree of relief in the tone of the dead Irene Boucher's brother-in-law.

'Right!' the Virginian answered as he swung down from his saddle. 'With some troopers from Fort St James.'

He trudged through the snow, going between Zeller and the sergeant who were still aiming their rifles at the wagon from which one of the Aaronites had spoken.

Dubois and Averill came in Steele's wake, the captain growling at the non-coms to check the other wagons.

'Just me and my wife here,' Mayne revealed morosely. And began to weep.

Snow had drifted around the wagons and it was still frozen, the rays of the sun not penetrating this far into the circle of rocks. So that the Virginian and two officers were able to climb up the crisp-surfaced hump and peer over the fastened tailgate. Saw little until Steele struck a match.

The elderly, grey haired Paul Mayne was huddled against a side of the Conestoga, almost entirely concealed by a mound of blankets so that just his head showed at the pinnacle. Immediately across the wagon bed from him his wife lay on her back: not covered up. Her eyes closed and her arms crossed at a chest that did not rise and fall with breathing.

There were two cartons of supplies and a keg of water at the front of the wagon.

Steele dropped the match into the snow just before

the flame was about to touch his gloved finger and thumb.

'Other wagons are empty, sir,' the sergeant reported.

And was ignored by the officers as Paul Mayne stemmed his tears and began to talk softly, in the darkness that Steele did not lighten with another match.

'The storm didn't seem to be so bad here. The padre said we were nearing journey's end. We were all eager to press on. But the horses weren't able to pull the padre's wagon more than a few yards up the slope. We all put our backs into it. It was her heart, I guess. Never was any sign it was weak before. She just keeled over. Without makin' a sound. But then my Gertrude never was one to complain.

'We couldn't shift the wagon any further up the slope. So the padre, he said we should leave three of them here and hitch the teams to the other two. I didn't see none of that. Just sat here with Gertrude, waitin' for her to die. Knew she would. But wanted it to be peaceful. Quiet like. And the padre said it would be okay for me to stay here with her. Left me some provisions. Said for me to follow on foot when I was ready and if the weather allowed.

'She went in the night. Without a sound. Without complaint. But I couldn't bring myself to leave her. Took the blankets off her and laid her out decent. Hoped the padre would send folks back to help me bury her. Can't do it myself. Blankets ain't been warmin' me for a long time. Cold as ice I am. Can't move a limb nor even a muscle. Against the faith to ask for help from folks who ain't Aaronites. Just have to hope the padre sends some help.'

'He's freezing to death, sir,' Averill whispered.

'Probably has frostbite already,' the general growled. 'Have the men light a fire, captain. Plenty of seasoned timber in the construction of these wagons.'

'No!' Mayne countermanded. 'You must not help me. The other soldiers who came by respected the Aaronite faith –'

'Other soldiers?' Averill rasped. 'When was this, mister?'

Despite the pain and misery and grief he was suffering, Paul Mayne's mind registered the desperation in the captain's tone.

'Maybe an hour or so after the padre led the others up into the pass. I could still move about some then. There was five of them. In a big hurry after I told them about the two wagons goin' up into the ridges. Seems the pass ain't open much after the snow comes. And they figured that if the wagons hadn't come back, then it was still open and them and their horses could get through. If they pressed on before much more snow fell.'

'They didn't hurt you. Or steal anything from you?' Dubois asked and there was a tone of excitement in his voice.

'No, sir. Only they weren't too friendly. But then they was real cold and real weary. Like they'd been in the saddle for a long time. I asked them if they'd seen anythin' of the folks that turned back, but they just rode off up into the pass without answerin'.'

The general and the captain moved down off the heap of frozen snow and held a low-voiced discussion before Averill began issuing orders.

'You still there, Mr Steele?' Mayne asked.

'Yes.'

'Tell them not to help me. I'd just as soon stay here and wait for my time to join Gertrude.'

'And the Horans and Miss Boucher, feller,' the Virginian told him. 'The Rycott boys, too.'

'They didn't make it?' There was a tone of gloom in his voice, but no sorrow. 'It was just after the storm started. Clinton Rycott said he was not goin' to risk the lives of his sons. Irene was afraid, too. And Bradley Horan was for turnin' back to wait for better weather. So the padre called a convocation. We was right in the middle of the plain by then. The wind howlin' and the snow hittin' us near horizontal. All of us save for Horan and my wife's sister was for pressin' on like the padre wanted. Rycott, too, after Grace Horan said she'd do whatever her husband wanted and they said they'd take the two boys with them. Horan said he'd make for the head of the valley and take shelter until the storm blew out. Then come after us. They didn't make it, uh?'

'No, feller. They didn't make it.'

'I prayed for them. Same as I prayed for the padre and the others to get through the pass. It is all the will of God.' He sighed and added: 'As was the death of the Indians by your hand.'

'You found them before the snow began?'

'And buried them.'

'The rifles?'

'The padre had Bradley Horan take them deep into the trees where they will never be found.'

'Sorry about your wife, Mr Mayne,' Steele said as he turned away from the rear of the wagon, the death of Corporal Grimes now explained. Horan had kept a Winchester and broken one of the Aaronite principles before he and his party died.

'You will tell them not to help me?' the man who was freezing to death called after him.

But the general's orders were already being carried

out. Six saddle horses had been hitched to the traces of the Mayne wagon and their former riders were engaged in digging the wheels of the Conestoga out of the frozen snow.

'Consider it best that the civilian should be taken back to the post as soon as possible, mister,' Dubois told the Virginian. 'Where he will be given medication in warmth and shelter. You are at liberty to return with the sergeant and his detail if you wish. Or to continue with the journey that brought you to the fort in the first place.'

'Reckoned I was free to do what I wanted after we found the dead soldier at the outcrop, general?'

Dubois showed a brief smile. 'Yes, of course you were. But at that time, there were still unanswered questions in your mind. Have they not now all been answered?'

'All except one, far as I'm concerned, general.'

'Which is?'

'Is it possible to get through the pass.'

The senior officer nodded and massaged his brow, as though tiredness approaching exhaustion was being felt as a headache.

'Lieutenant March and his deserters had no desire to go east. They could have made good time in that direction, but it is too obvious. With a good chance they would be captured. To the south at this time of year there is a vast tract of mountains a man would be an utter fool to try to cross. I think they attempted to go west at first. And they could have made it that way if the storm did not happen. But they were driven back and decided to make for Three Peaks Pass having the good fortune – from their points of view – to stumble upon the wagon and its supplies at the outcrop. It is the only explanation for why the deserters remained in the area for so long.'

Steele crossed to where the horses waited and Dubois trailed him while Averill urged the work party to speed up the snow clearing chore.

'You have a reason for not returning along the east trail, mister?' Dubois asked as Steele got astride his gelding.

'Just that I rode in from that way, general. And I don't like going over old ground.'

'Nor being under my command?'

'No offence, general, but the thing I liked least when I was in the army was taking orders.'

A weary nod. 'You have never failed to make it plain that you are a loner, Mr Steele. A man alone.'

'Never claim to be somebody I'm not, general. But there are occasions when being what I am gives me the edge.'

CHAPTER FOURTEEN

AS THE night advanced, the cold got worse because each yard the gelding carried Adam Steele took man and mount to a higher altitude.

Once around the curve of the trail that rose out of the encirclement of rocky heights, the grade was less steep but constantly unremitting in its demands upon stamina. Not least because the snow that was almost a foot deep had a heavy crusting of frost so that it did not powder easily in front of the gelding's legs.

After perhaps an hour, the Virginian got out of the saddle and led the horse by the reins. Both to allow the animal a respite from carrying the burden of his weight, and to generate body heat from the exertion of ploughing through the snow.

Thirty minutes later he saw sign in the snow ahead. The ruts left by wheelrims and the impressions of hooves and booted feet. When he reached the point where they first showed on the otherwise undisturbed surface of the snow, he by turns flapped his arms across his chest and vigorously massaged his face to rub off the frost crystals clinging to his bristles.

The two Conestogas with the extra horses in the traces had reached this point when the snowstorm ended and the faster moving army deserters were not far behind them. The morning sun had melted the snow a little, so that the edges of the impressions were no longer clear cut.

From where he stood, flapping his arms and now stamping his feet, the Virginian could see why the pass had been given both the Indian and the anglicised names.

One peak towered above him immediately to his left. On the other side of a deep chasm some quarter mile wide, a second mountain reared to the right. Ahead, due north and perhaps three miles away, a third ridge appeared, over this distance, to block the way and deny that there was indeed a pass through the mountains here.

Not only the biting cold of the still air and the moon-bright whiteness of the snow contributed to the appropriateness of the Indian idea that the pass was a kind of hell, far removed from that threatened by fire and brimstone preachers. For there were, too, the grotesque formations of the rocks which had been sculptured by the eroding action of harsh weather over many millions of years.

On the faces of the mountains and in the shapes of outcrops – even in the manner in which ancient rock falls had scattered giant boulders down into the pass – a man with imagination could see countless impressions of weird and awesome tableaus. Men and women, alone and in groups. Animals and birds. All of them gruesomely ugly. Frozen in attitudes of fiendish laughter or hysterical torment. Locked in mortal combat or escaping from a terrible threat.

Some of them not frozen, Steele saw as he began to lead the gelding over the sign made by the Aaronites and the deserters. For with a change of perspective, the moonlight gleamed on the rocks and cast the shadows in a slightly different direction, causing a fresh image to appear. Sometimes something entirely different – while here and there it appeared that the solid rock representation of a nightmarish creature was sluggishly stirring.

'Sure is one hell of a place,' the Virginian growled and drew no response from the gelding. But was answered by the echo of his own words which, despite the lowness of his tone, bounced back up at him from the depths of the chasm to the right.

He trudged on through the snowscape on which no plantlife existed: beyond the end of the chasm, and then twisted and turned among outcrops and rock falls, following the frost crusted sign that despite the frequent turns to get around obstacles led him ultimately toward the north-west which was apparently the only way to avoid the high ridge which at first had seemed to block off the pass.

And he was almost at the western end of the ridge, the moon paling in the grey light of approaching dawn when he saw the two Conestogas. One of them tilted at a crazy angle with a front corner in the air, its canvas cover gone and its timbers partially burned. The other upright and seemingly undamaged.

Nearby was a large group of horses, huddled together for mutual warmth under a cliff at the end of the ridge.

Steele could see no sign of human life. But he could see the tracks left by people which led away from the wagons and horses and went up and over a great heap of snow that filled the gap between the end of the ridge and the sheer drop into another chasm to the west.

He slid the Colt Hartford from the boot and had to use a great deal of force to bring back the frozen hammer. And he approached the wagons with the rifle canted to his shoulder, gloved hand fisted tightly around the frame – anxious the firing mechanism did not freeze again.

Full dawn came, but the high ground to the east still hid the sun when he was close enough to make an estimate of the number of disconsolate looking horses. Certainly more than the twenty animals which had been split into two teams of ten to haul the heavily laden Conestogas through the pass. So probably twenty-six to include the mounts of the deserters.

Closer still, he saw that the snow had not drifted to block the way for the wagons or even the men astride horses at the end of the ridge. Instead, a minor avalanche had slid hundreds of tons of snow down off the high ground.

Without careful study at close range, it was not possible to see how many people had left sign of their trek on foot away from the wagons and over the heap of snow.

The burnt-out wagon was the only evidence of possible trouble – and this might simply mean that it had been ignited to keep warm: not be an indication of violence.

Steele had to lead his horse over a half mile of open, gently sloping ground to reach the wagons. And as he closed the distance he was constantly tensed for a sound or movement to warn of danger. While he was more aware than at any time during the night that he was not alone in the pass. For although an occasional backward glance had never revealed any sign of

General Gerald Dubois and his men from Fort St James, he did not doubt they were somewhere on the trail behind him.

And he thought of them now because of the danger they represented to him. If the deserters were watching him from the undamaged wagon, they might well accept him as an innocent lone traveller. Initially, at least. But should a bunch of uniformed men appear behind him . . . ?

The first shaft of sunlight lanced down from above the high ground to the east, dazzlingly bright as it reflected off the snow.

And a man said: 'You crazy or something, mister?'

Steele halted and made to swing the Colt Hartford down from his shoulder.

A rifle barrel jutted out through a tear in the wagon canvas. And the man who aimed it rasped:

'We all got enough problems without shooting at each other, wouldn't you say?'

His voice and perhaps a kick here and there caused other men in the wagon to be roused from sleep. And then come awake with grunts and coughs and questions.

Steele steadied the Colt Hartford back against his shoulder. And drawled: 'No denying you've got me cold, feller.'

'Why I didn't tell you to freeze, mister. Stand out there like you are for long and you could do just that.'

Men began to emerge from over the tailgate of the wagon and drop to the snow. Three men in their mid-thirties and another who looked to be not yet twenty. All wearing army greatcoats. One of the older men with sergeant chevrons on his sleeve. They all had holstered guns at their waists and the non-com was carrying a Springfield rifle which he held in a one-handed grip, aimed casually in Steele's direction but not at him.

The gun barrel was withdrawn from the tear in the canvas and Lieutenant March came out of the wagon: canting the rifle to his shoulder in the same manner as Steele – who tugged on the reins of the gelding and moved closer to the group.

'Lieutenant March on patrol from Fort St James,' the forty year old, heavily built, bushily moustached officer said coldly, his green eyes filled with suspicion. 'You know the post?'

'Heard of it, lieutenant. Feller sharing a wagon with his dead wife at the south end of the pass mentioned you.'

'Get a fire going and start breakfast, Averill,' March ordered and the young trooper who bore no family resemblance to his brother moved toward the flame-charred wagon.

Suspicion was more deeply inscribed on the heavily bristled faces of the sergeant and two troopers than that of the officer.

'You'll join us, mister?'

'Grateful to you.'

'Started out to be a routine patrol.' He leaned his rifle against a rear wheel of the wagon and scooped up snow to rub it to water against the flesh of his face. 'But came under attack by a group of people on a wagon just like this one. Lost a man.'

'I saw, lieutenant. A man, two women and two kids.'

The non-com seemed about to speak, but March got in first. 'Hell of a thing,' he said bitterly. 'Snowing so we could hardly see a thing. The corporal was hit before we knew there was anybody around. We thought it was a bunch of renegade hostiles attacking us until it was all over.

'One of the women was still alive. Told us she thought we were the Indians. Seems they'd had trouble with them before. Told us there were five other wagons heading north for the pass. Tried to catch up with them. Warn the folks aboard the way is almost always blocked by snow this time of year.

'But they found that out for themselves. Taken off on foot. Hope to hell they made it.'

He looked bleakly toward the heap of snow with the tracks in it and shook his head as if reflecting that it was probable they did not get far.

'What happened to the other wagon?' Steele asked as smoke began to rise from it.

'Got bogged down. I had it doused with kerosene and burned. To warm the men and myself and hopeful the smoke would be seen and bring back the folks who abandoned the wagons and horses. But it was a faint hope, I have to admit, mister. Seems they're some kind of religious sect who won't accept help from outsiders and consider everything good and bad to be the will of the Lord.'

'Gathered that from talking to the man whose wife died.'

'Wouldn't have you do anything for him either, uh?'

'No.'

There was an interruption to the exchange of lies and half-truths when Averill came back to the undamaged wagon to get provisions for breakfast out of it.

'But you ain't crazy are you, mister?' the sergeant said, without shifting his narrow eyed gaze from the south – peering out over the tracks in the brilliantly white snow to where they first showed at the side of a grotesquely shaped outcrop. 'Like the lieutenant asked when he first saw you?'

'Sergeant Power!' March snapped grimly, and it was obvious the officer feared the non-com was in danger of revealing this was not a routine patrol out of Fort St James.

The young Averill went back to the fire in the charred wagon, carrying a bundle of supplies. And while the other two troopers continued their watch for trouble from the south, Power became respectful toward the officer.

'Beg pardon, sir. But this civilian bein' in the pass at this time of year. Trailin' the religious folks and all. It's gotten to be a real busy place.'

March nodded. 'I take the sergeant's point, Mr . . . ?'

'Steele, lieutenant.'

'Mr Steele. You are in territory which comes within the jurisdiction of St James. And it is my duty to enquire your business here. As much for your own safety as to –' He showed a wan smile '– have something to write in my report when I return to the post.'

'Just passing through, lieutenant.'

'To where?'

The Virginian showed a brief smile of his own. 'To heaven, if the Indian name for this pass means anything.'

Power made a sound of impatience and Steele knew he was still alive only because March retained his authority over the deserters. And the Virginian went on evenly:

'I'm a drifter. Go where the trails lead me.'

Power was set to voice a grim toned comment, but March spoke first.

'The only regular trail in this whole piece of country leads to the post, Mr Steele.'

The Virginian made his new smile sardonic and kept it in place longer. 'That's what an old timer furtrapper told me a week or so ago. No reflection on you fellers choosing to be in the army. But I served my time in the war. Not the best of times for me. Ever since, I've tried to steer clear of the military.'

This new half truth about his feelings had the effect he had hoped for. There was an abrupt easing of tension within Power and the two troopers. But March spoke quickly to ensure they did not blurt out enthusiastic sympathy with the civilian's opinion of army life.

'No offence taken, Mr Steele. It would be a dull world if everyone were the same.' Then he raised his voice. 'How's breakfast coming along, trooper?'

'Coffee's bubblin' already, sir!' Averill called.

March gestured for Steele to lead the way and he did so, after easing forward the hammer of the Colt Hartford, sliding the rifle back in the boot and hitching the reins of the gelding to a rear wheel of the Conestoga. The non-com tossed his Springfield into the back of the wagon but all the men had revolvers in their holsters and the Virginian experienced an itch between the shoulder blades as he trudged through the snow ahead of them.

The burnt-out wagon still smelled of the fire from a distance. But close to, the aromas of brewing coffee and frying bacon filled the morning air. Just the canvas cover and one corner of the tilted wagon had been entirely consumed by flames. Elsewhere the fire had died or been doused before it could engulf the rig. Breakfast was being cooked over a fire the young trooper had lit in a small stove which had once belonged to an Aaronite family.

Averill had set out six plates, mugs and eating irons

which were also of Aaronite origin.

'Guess if the civilians make it through the pass, they won't thank us for burning one of their wagons,' the officer said. 'Seem to have taken only the supplies they could carry. With the intention of coming back here to get what they can salvage after the snow melts.'

It was not until he was within range of the heat from the stove that Steele realized how cold he was from the long night's trek into the pass. And perhaps fear also contributed to the threat of trembling he struggled to stem.

The young trooper gave him a mug of steaming coffee and in gripping it with both hands and sipping from it, he beat the threat. Asked:

'What's your next move, lieutenant?'

'Wait it out here,' March answered without needing to take the time to think – as the men peered at him over the rims of their mugs. 'Figure a patrol will be sent out from the post to look for us . . . you didn't see any other patrol to the south did you, Mr Steele?'

'No, lieutenant.'

March nodded and his men appeared to believe the civilian as readily as the officer.

'Give them until midday to show and if they don't, have to send a man back to report, I guess.' He squinted at the sky in the east. 'Unless the sun gets hot enough to melt the snow so we can get through.' Now he shook his head. 'Don't figure those folks have a chance of still being alive. But it's our duty to check.'

Averill was ladling out bacon and beans.

Steele said: 'One of the main reasons I didn't like the army, lieutenant. It always seemed they wanted me to do what didn't appeal to me.'

There were some grunts of understanding.

March growled: 'There's no place for that brand of individualism in the army, mister.'

And Steele wondered if, had he not known these men were deserters, he would have detected the almost imperceptible tone of bitterness in the lieutenant's tone.

They ate breakfast in silence, warmed much more by the fire and food than the rising sun. While the uniformed men cast several surreptitious glances toward the south. Steele was careful not to reveal that he saw the men's interest in the south as anything more than eagerness for a relief patrol to get here.

And began to suspect the motives of March, Power and the two veteran troopers – he had the impression that young Miles Averill was totally out of his depth in the whole situation. But the other four were in control of themselves. Three of them prepared to go along with the fourth for as long as they considered he was handling things to their satisfaction.

All of them believed Steele's lies, but in telling the lies the Virginian now knew he had gained nothing except time. Time which would start to run out fast from the moment General Gerald Dubois and his men showed in the pass. For the men with whom he was sharing breakfast were caught in a trap with the way out to the north almost certainly blocked and the strong possibility, in the minds of the deserters, that a force of men was closing in on them from the south.

So a civilian hostage might just be what they needed to escape the trap – and if they succeeded, the hostage would have outlived his usefulness to them.

'Figure you're feeling a lot better now, Mr Steele,' March said as the meal came to an end. 'Can't be a much better way to work up an appetite than a night trip through Three Peaks Pass.'

'Can't recall a time when breakfast was more welcome, lieutenant. And I reckon that with a full belly I'm ready to make a try to get over that heap of snow.'

The Virginian was looking at the officer who showed no physical reaction to what he heard, nor to the sudden return of tension which Steele sensed gripped the other men.

'Can't allow you to do that, mister. Far too dangerous.' March turned his head to glance toward the snow blockage between the end of the ridge and the chasm. Made to look back at Steele but did a double take – his expression altering to a scowl of fear.

Steele and the others saw this and swung their intrigued attention in the same direction.

Glimpsed a figure up on the crest of the snow. Saw him stagger and throw his arms to the sides. Heard a rifle shot from the south.

The man up on the snow fell.

The soldiers around Steele began to curse – except for Miles Averill who started to whimper.

A fusillade of rifle shots thudded bullets into the burnt-out wagon.

Steele drawled: 'Examples prove nut cases, lieutenant,' as he recognized the scrawny figure of Aaron Curtain sprawled in the snow.

CHAPTER FIFTEEN

THE VIRGINIAN and the deserters had all pitched full length into the snow behind the cover of the tilted Conestoga as the bullets pitted the timbers of the wagon and rang against the metal of its construction to ricochet into the sunlit morning air.

March and Miles Averill on one side of Steele, close to the stove, and Power and the two veteran troopers on the other side.

Each soldier clawed for the Army Colt in his holster.

Steele rolled on to his right side and drew up his right leg: reached in through the gaping slit in his pants to slide the knife from the boot sheath – the object of his moves concealed by his leg and the snow.

Another fusillade of shots sprayed the wagon with bullets and in its wake the voices of men and the thud of hooves could be heard.

'The bastard set us up!' Power roared as he got the revolver clear of his holster.

Steele had his back to the sergeant and the veteran

troopers. Was facing the lieutenant and Averill and was certain, too, that he was facing death. For both the officer and the young trooper had their Colts drawn and cocked – one snarling and the other weeping.

The Virginian made his choice of which man he would try to take with him – and braced a boot on the side of the wagon to give momentum to his lunge at March – right arm swinging with the blade of the knife showing from the fist of his gloved hand.

More bullets hit the wagon.

The crack of the Colt in Averill's double-handed grip sounded insignificant against the volley of rifle fire.

The shell from the revolver went over Steele's lunging form and took the shocked Sergeant Power in the chest: left of centre.

At the same instant as Steele's elbow knocked March's Colt off target and he stabbed the knife to the hilt into the officer's terror-widened left eye.

Miles Averill was wailing like a grieving widow now, his hands trembling as he pulled back the hammer on his Colt.

Revolver shots were sounding among the deeper cracks of rifles to maintain a constant barrage against the wagon.

Steele released his grip on the killing knife and scooped up the dead officer's ready cocked Colt. Hurled himself over on to his back to swing the revolver to aim in the opposite direction.

One of the veteran troopers was writhing in agony with a misshapen ricochet imbedded at the centre of a bloody wound in his temple.

The other was whirling away in shock from the sight of the dead Power and the wounded trooper. But intent on blasting a shot at Miles Averill for the treacherous act of killing one of his own.

The youngster fired first, but in his trembling hands the shot went high and wide.

Steele squeezed off the next shot and the bullet tunnelled on a rising trajectory through the head of the man – entering his flesh between the jaw and throat. He was in a half squat when he took the bullet, the impact of which acted to unfold him almost upright.

He was seen by the soldiers charging up the slope and a volley of shots cracked toward him – blasted bloody chunks of flesh away from his head before he fell.

'I never wanted this!' Miles Averill shrieked as the injured trooper slumped into unconsciousness or death. And Steele instinctively rolled to get sight of the young trooper at the sound of his voice. 'I had to go along with them or they'd have killed me!'

The cavalry charge was maintained, the horses slowed by the deep snow and the upgrade: but the gunfire as constant as ever.

'Honest to God!' Averill continued, his voice rising to a shrill pitch. 'I ain't no deserter! But what could I do?'

He started to rise, the gun falling from his hands as he made to thrust his arms high in surrender.

Steele rolled and lunged into another dive across the snow, arms curled to clutch the lower legs of the hysterical young trooper – made contact and used his shoulders to topple him.

'Listen to . . .'

Miles Averill's shrieked plea was curtailed as another fusillade of gunfire blasted through the crystal clear air. From close enough for Steele to smell the taint of exploded powder in his nostrils.

The soldier whose legs he clutched was abruptly full length on the compacted snow, with a blossoming stain of crimson on the whiteness to either side of his head and torso.

Steele saw this, felt the death spasm in Averill's legs and released his grip. Heard the thud of hooves and equine snorts. And remained inert, face down on the cold snow – tensed to experience the impact of bullets tearing into him from close range. Fired by cavalry-men keyed up to kill.

But there were no more shots. Mounts were halted at the front and rear of the tilted wagon and along its side. And a dozen grim-faced men clutching smoking guns peered down at the bullet shattered corpses sprawled on the bloodstained snow.

'Damnit, sir, we hit Steele,' Corporal Zeller rasped.

'Fortunes of war,' Dubois responded flatly. 'He found out too late he was in a situation where force of numbers was to win the day.'

'If no one's still trigger happy, it's not too late, general,' the Virginian growled.

'Damnit, he ain't dead!' Zeller blurted. He still carried the company pennant.

Steele rose on to all fours and then to his feet: saw surprise but no relief in the weary faces of the two officers and men who were still mounted in an arc on three sides of him.

'Third mistake that was made this morning,' he said evenly.

'One was the man up there,' Dubois allowed and seemed about to point at where Aaron Curtain lay on the heap of snow. But then he merely gestured with his head, as if he feared he would topple with exhaustion from the saddle if he let go of the horn with either hand. 'We had been in position for thirty minutes, Mr Steele. Awaiting the moment to commence the charge. It is my responsibility. I ordered the sharpshooter to fire. On the assumption the man was a lookout who had spotted us.'

'The other mistake, sir?' Captain Averill asked, finally able to tear his gaze away from the bullet-riddled body and head of his kid brother. There was a catch in his voice. 'Does it concern my brother?'

'He was an unwilling member of the group of deserters,' the Virginian answered and wondered as he revealed this if it was better for the officer to know. Then decided he didn't care about the captain's feelings – he owed it to the young trooper that the truth be known. 'If he hadn't pretended to be with them, they'd have killed him. He kept me from being killed. And was trying to tell you when –'

'We were a troop engaged in a charge,' the surviving Averill cut in. 'Attacking a group who we had to assume were all intent upon killing us. There was no time or opportunity to take into account possible side issues.'

'That is precisely right, captain,' Dubois agreed. 'No soldier under my command has reason to question anything he did during this action. Have the men load the dead on their own mounts and prepare to leave. Abandon the serviceable wagon, but bring the team horses. Where are you going, Mr Steele?'

This last was snapped out in a tone of harsher authority: toward the back of the Virginian who was trudging through the snow toward the base of the heap on which the old man was sprawled.

'You mind to your army business and I'll mind to mine, general,' Steele called back.

'I intend to send men through the north section of the pass to . . .'

Steele shut out the rest of what the general was shouting to him. Reached the base of the snow slide and started up it. But the sun, the warmth of which he was not aware of, had started to melt the snow. And he was only halfway to his objective when he sank down to his waist and could go no further.

The voice of the Aaronite padre reached him as little more than a scratching sound on the silence over a distance of twenty yards.

'Soon we all will be dead. It is God's will.'

'The others who were with you?' the Virginian called. 'Your daughter and the rest?'

'An area of ice we failed to see in the darkness. All of them slithered to their deaths. I was spared. To return to the place where we started, I thought. To lead others of the faith on a journey that would not be doomed. But I was mistaken. It is the will of God!'

His voice seemed to be getting stronger.

'Where are you hit?' Steele called.

'It matters not! For I know I am doomed like the others! None of us worthy in the all-seeing eyes of our creator to . . .'

There was an ominous crunching sound which did not curtail what Aaron Curtain was intoning, but masked it to the ears of Adam Steele.

Then the section of the crest of the heap of snow on which the old man lay began to slide. Not melted any faster than any area of snow on which the sun shone. But caused to move by the slight weight of the frail form sprawled upon it.

The Virginian was as helpless as the more distantly placed soldiers to do anything. Could see the padre's mouth moving and guessed he was still allowing that the Almighty was right to claim the lives of all the Aaronites who came west on the wagons.

Then the form was lost amid a cloud of snow as he was tipped over the rim of the chasm. There was little noise now. Certainly not a scream from the tumbling figure. Next, total silence.

Until Steele turned and struggled back down the treacherous slope of melting snow.

Dubois ordered the men to continue with their chores as the Virginian returned to the wagons. Captain Averill had never interrupted his personal task of attending to the transport of the corpse of his brother.

'Well, Mr Steele?' the senior officer said as he sipped coffee from what might well have been the mug of a dead man. 'Was he able to tell you anything before that happened?'

'Yes, general. You've no need to send men further into the pass. All those who went with him are dead.'

'A tragedy.'

'Reckon so, general. And that was the . . .

. . . FINAL CURTAIN.'*

* On this Adam Steele story. But another will open shortly.